Holly reached up through the leaves. The sensible part of her brain was telling her that this was just one of Miranda's jokes. But then her fingers touched something smooth and flat.

'Oh!' She took hold and pulled it down from its secret nest in the tree.

The envelope was about thirty centimetres by twenty centimetres, and very fat in the middle.

Peter took the envelope from Holly and felt all over it.

'What do you think is in it?' asked Miranda. She gave the top of the envelope a prod.

The flap lifted and the mouth of the envelope gaped. Holly leaned over Peter's shoulder as all three of them tried to see what was inside.

Peter brought the bundle out. It was a thick wad of twenty pound notes.

'There must be hundreds of pounds here!' gasped Miranda. 'Why would anyone leave an envelope full of cash up a tree?'

## The Mystery Kids series

1 Spy-Catchers!
2 Lost and Found
3 Treasure Hunt
4 The Empty House
5 Smugglers Bay
6 Funny Money
7 Blackmail!
8 Mystery Weekend
9 Wrong Number
10 Hostage!
11 Box of Tricks
12 Kidnap!

# THE MYSTERY KiDS

# Blackmail!

## Fiona Kelly

Hodder
Children's
Books

a division of Hodder Headline plc

**Special thanks to Allan Frewin Jones**

Copyright © 1995 Ben M. Baglio
Created by Ben M. Baglio
London W6 0HE

First published in Great Britain in 1996
by Hodder Children's Books

A Catalogue record for this book is
available from the British Library

ISBN 0 340 65356 6

Typeset by Hewer Text Composition Services, Edinburgh
Printed and bound in Great Britain by
Mackays of Chatham PLC, Chatham, Kent

Hodder Children's Books
a division of Hodder Headline plc
338 Euston Road
London NW1 3BH

# Contents

1   John Raven: Secret Agent                1
2   Strange behaviour                      14
3   Elementary                             26
4   Money trouble                          37
5   Creepy Crawly                          50
6   Something nasty in the post            63
7   Conclusive evidence                    76
8   Discovered                             85
9   The drummer boy's secret               99
10  Where is Maurice Harty?               112
11  The Battle of Benedict Avenue         124
12  All wrapped up                        134
13  Case closed                           143

# John Raven:
# Secret Agent

Secret Agent Holly Adams edged her way along the ledge. She glanced down. Between her feet the sheer drop ended in hard paving-stones far, far below.

'Don't look down!' called her companion, Secret Agent Peter Hamilton.

'I wasn't,' said Holly.

'Yes you were,' said Peter.

Holly glared at him. 'This is no time for an argument,' she said. 'What am I supposed to say to the Coordinator if I fall off and break my neck? Sorry, ma'am, but I lost my footing 'cos I was chatting to Peter?'

Peter looked thoughtfully at her as she sidled to the end of the ledge.

'Who said the Coordinator was a woman?' he asked. 'I don't remember agreeing that.'

'Miranda and I decided last night,' said

Holly. 'We took a vote. The Coordinator is a woman.'

'Wait a minute,' said Peter. 'How could you vote on it? I wasn't even there.'

'What difference would that have made?' asked Holly. 'There's two of us and only one of you, so you'd have been outvoted anyway.' She gave him a reassuring smile. 'Don't worry, we took your opinions into account.'

'Hmm,' muttered Peter. 'Before ignoring them.'

'Exactly,' said Holly. 'And now, if you don't mind, I've got to think of a way of getting across this gap.' It wasn't a particularly wide gap, but, Holly thought, a person had to be extra careful when the slightest mistake might send them plummeting to their doom. After all, what would a passer-by make of it if a secret agent suddenly went splat on the pavement at their feet?

She was on the point of transferring her weight when the door burst open.

'I've seen him!' Miranda yelled as she came catapulting into the room. 'I've *seen* him!'

Holly lost her footing on the windowsill

and disappeared behind the desk with a shriek.

Peter nearly fell off his chair in shock as Miranda seemed to explode in all directions, her round cheeks bright red and her long blonde hair flying. Miranda Hunt was a very loud sort of person at the best of times, and when she got excited, people were reminded of fire-alarms and police sirens and foghorns.

'You big twit!' Holly said, her grey eyes appearing over the back of the desk, her long brown hair falling over her face. 'We were trying to work out what John Raven would do next!'

'If Miranda had started shouting at him, he'd have fallen off the ledge, I expect,' said Peter.

Holly was talking about Secret Agent John Raven, the intrepid hero of the Mystery Kids' favourite TV show, *Spyglass*. Every week the three of them would be glued to the screen while John Raven thwarted the plans of an endless number of fiendish villains. At the end of last night's episode, John Raven had been perched on a ledge high up on a skyscraper.

If he went back he would walk straight into the enemy's deadly neuron blaster. If he went forward he had to jump to another ledge to escape. If Miranda had suddenly appeared, yelling at the top of her voice, he would probably have reacted the same way as Holly, and that would have been the end of John Raven – and of *Spyglass*.

'But I've seen him!' wailed Miranda, her arms flailing for emphasis. 'In the park!'

'Who?' asked Holly, getting out from behind the desk.

'*Him!*' Miranda was almost gibbering with excitement. 'John Raven! In the park! As large as life! Walking along! With a coat on!'

Peter flicked his light brown hair out of his eyes and looked pityingly at her.

'I don't know how to break this to you, Miranda,' he said, giving her a really superior look as he sat curled up in their swivel arm-chair. 'But John Raven isn't a real person. He's only on TV!'

Without another word, Miranda leapt at him, grabbed the arm of the chair and spun it with all her strength. Peter clung on grimly as the walls of their office whirled in front of his eyes.

'I know that!' yelled Miranda. 'I didn't mean I saw John Raven himself. I mean I saw the actor who *plays* John Raven. I saw Maurice Harty!'

'You didn't!' gasped Holly.

'I did!' Miranda said with a wide grin.

Peter managed to bring the revolving chair to a halt.

'Where?' he asked.

'In Belair Park,' said Miranda.

'When?'

'Oh, a week ago last Tuesday,' said Miranda. 'I just couldn't be bothered to tell you about it before now.' She waved her arms in the air. 'Just *now*, you nit! Five minutes ago. I ran all the way here.'

'Here' was the Mystery Kids' 'office'. A small room in the house in Highgate, North London, where Peter and his father lived.

Holly had come up with the idea of forming a secret agency with Miranda in response to *Spyglass* and a beloved book called *Harriet the Spy*. Holly had read Harriet's adventures over and over again when she had been a little younger. Harriet lived in New York City and spent all her time spying on her friends and neighbours and writing everything down in a notebook.

Not that Holly and Miranda were going round snooping on people, but, as Holly said, they did live in London, and a city the size of London must be teeming with foreign agents and secret intrigues that needed to be investigated.

That was how they came to meet up with Peter whose hobby, writing down car number plates, seemed very suspicious to them at first. But even after they had learned that Peter's hobby was perfectly innocent, it was through meeting him that the three of them came to solve a *real* crime. A robbery at the bank where Holly's mother worked!

They even got their photos in the newspapers. It was the headline *MYSTERY KIDS FOIL BANK ROBBERY* that had given them a name for their agency: the Mystery Kids!

But that had been several exciting adventures ago and now they had their own room in Peter's house, with a desk and a filing cabinet and a large map of London on the wall. Suspicious goings-on were marked with bright red pins. Red for mystery!

Not that they were involved in anything mysterious right then, which was why Holly and Peter were taking time out to try and guess how John Raven would escape last night's cliffhanger when Miranda came charging in.

Holly gazed at the pinboard above their desk. In pride of place was a large colour photograph cut from a recent Sunday newspaper supplement. It had accompanied an interview with Maurice Harty, the actor who played John Raven on TV. It was from this interview that they had discovered, to their amazement, that the Harty family (Maurice, his wife Edwina, who was also a successful actor, and their seven year old daughter Bethany) lived in Highgate, North London – just like the Mystery Kids themselves!

They had all been on the lookout for him ever since, but nothing had been seen of him until now.

'Let's get over there!' yelled Holly. 'We can get his autograph. Maybe he'll even give me an interview for *The Tom-tom*.' *The Tom-tom* was the lower-school magazine which Holly and Miranda co-edited at the Thomas Petheridge School, which all three of them attended.

'He'll be gone,' said the ever-practical Peter. 'We'll be wasting our time.' He looked at Miranda. 'I don't suppose you thought to follow him and find out where he lives?'

'No,' admitted Miranda. 'I was too excited. I took one look at him and came running over to tell you.'

'You could at least have got an autograph first,' sighed Holly.

'Well, excuse me for wanting to share the news with you,' said Miranda. 'I thought you'd be thrilled to bits.'

'We are,' said Holly. She gave Miranda a big hug. 'We're totally, completely and utterly thrilled to bits! What did he look like? Did he look the same? What was he wearing? How tall was he? My mum says people look taller in TV than they are in real life. I always thought he'd be really tall in real life. Does he look the same?'

'Wait a minute! Wait a minute!' Miranda

gasped under the torrent of Holly's questions. 'I only saw him for, like, thirty seconds. I was walking along that path near the main road, and he was going across that diagonal path. You know, the one that takes you to Hamlet Road. He was walking in the opposite direction to me.'

Peter eyed her dubiously. 'Are you sure it was him?'

'Of course I am!' Miranda ran over to the wall map and found the small patch of green that was Belair Park. 'He was walking along here.' Her finger traced a slanted line across the park. 'From the main road, see?'

'From the direction of the underground station,' said Holly, leaning over her shoulder.

'Going home from work, I bet,' said Peter, leaning on Miranda's other shoulder as the three of them studied the wall map. 'It's the right time of day for someone to be going home.'

'Maybe he'll be there tomorrow,' Miranda said as she gradually sank under the combined weight of Peter and Holly's arms on her shoulders.

9

Holly and Peter looked at each other over Miranda's head.

'Are you thinking what I'm thinking?' asked Holly.

'I don't know,' said Peter. 'What are you thinking?'

'I'm thinking that if a person came home from the TV studio at a particular time and by a particular route *today* . . .'

'Then he might well do the same tomorrow,' Miranda finished. 'And if three other people just happened to be in the park at the right time, they might get to meet him!'

Peter and Holly grinned and slapped their hands together above Miranda's head with a triumphant shout of '*Yesss!*'

'You're sure it was him?' Peter asked Miranda.

'Yes!' Miranda howled, grabbing him by the lapels and shaking him. 'How many more times? It was *him!*'

'Shhh!' hissed Holly. 'People are looking.'

They were sitting on a bench in Belair Park. It was the following afternoon. The three of them had run like mad at the end of school, panicking that they might arrive too late and miss him. Peter's protests that they were a lot earlier than when Miranda had seen him yesterday fell on deaf ears.

'What if he's early and we miss him because we're strolling along wasting time?' Miranda had asked.

Their bench was a little way along the lower of the two main paths. This one ran parallel to the main street. The other made its wiggly way into a small patch of trees before coming out into the open again at the far corner of the park.

They could see the underground station on the corner of the street. Every now and then a flood of people would come out and disperse in all directions.

'He's late,' said Peter, looking at his watch. 'If it *was* him.'

'Perhaps he's been held up at the office,' Miranda said hopefully.

'What *office*?' said Peter. 'He's an actor. Actors don't work in offices. They work on sets and out on location and stuff like that.'

'Perhaps he's been held up at the set, then,' insisted Miranda. 'He'll be here. Stop fretting.'

'Maybe there was a phone call just as he was leaving,' said Holly. 'A call from Hollywood.' Her imagination began to gather speed as she put on a bad American accent. 'Hello? Mr Harty. *The* Mr Harty? I'm calling you on behalf of a very important movie director. My boss was wondering if you'd like to come over and star in a new film he's working on? *Spyglass, The Movie*. You would? Great!' Holly grinned at her two friends.

'Wouldn't that be amazing? A *Spyglass* film?'

'Yeah,' said Miranda. 'It'd be brilliant.' She looked thoughtful for a moment. 'I've just realised something,' she said, looking at Holly. 'Wouldn't it be amazing if your last name was Wood? Because, if it was—'

Peter groaned and Holly shook her head in mock despair.

'No, listen,' Miranda persisted. 'Don't you get it? If your first name was Holly, which it is, and your last name was Wood, you'd be—'

'Isn't that him?' interrupted Peter, staring towards the underground station. There were several people at the zebra crossing. One was a tall man in a grey coat.

12

'Oh, crumbs!' Holly gasped, her hands up to her mouth. 'It isn't. Is it? It can't be. Can it? It *is*! It's *him*!'

There was no doubt in any of their minds as the tall man strode across the road and came into the park.

Beyond any shred of a doubt, Maurice Harty, the man who played Secret Agent John Raven, their greatest hero in the whole world, was walking right towards them.

**Strange behaviour**

Maurice Harty walked into the park with his hands in his coat pocket and his head down. He took the diagonal path, walking very quickly, as though he was desperate to get home as fast as possible.

The heads of the three friends swivelled round as six wide-open eyes followed him along the path.

'Quick,' whispered Holly. 'Do something!'

'Like what?' whispered Peter.

'I don't know. *Something.*'

'Why are we whispering?' asked Miranda.

'It is him,' said Peter. He glanced round at the others. 'Do you think he looks as if he'd be pleased to be jumped on by three fans?'

'Not particularly,' said Holly. 'He looks as if he's really in a hurry. Perhaps we could follow him and find out where he lives.

Then we could write him a polite letter. We could tell him we're his greatest fans, and – Miranda, where are you going?'

'To get an autograph,' said Miranda. 'You two can sit here and talk about it if you like, but I'm not missing out on a chance like this.'

'It's probably better if only one of us goes up to him,' said Peter. 'Miranda?' he called. 'Be polite.'

'Of course!' Miranda called back over her shoulder as she broke into a trot and gathered speed across the grass towards the actor.

The other two hung over the back of the park bench, watching as she neared Maurice Harty.

'If he stops and shows any sign of being happy to chat,' said Holly, 'we'll go over as well, OK?'

'*If* he stops,' Peter said dubiously. Maurice Harty was making his way across the park at quite a speed.

'Excuse me,' Miranda called, using her extra-special ultra-polite Sunday-best voice. She ran on to the path and came trotting up alongside the tall man.

He glanced down at her. Yes, there were

the intelligent brown eyes, the finely chis-elled cheekbones, the sweep of black hair, the strong chin and determined mouth of John Raven.

He looked at his watch. 'Ten past four,' he said, speeding up.

'Er, no,' said Miranda, trotting to keep up with him. 'That's not what I wanted.' She beamed him a smile. '"Just call me the early bird",' she quoted. That was one of John Raven's catchphrases. He'd use it after cornering a foreign agent. 'The early bird catches the worm.'

'Go away!' snapped the man.

Miranda almost tripped over her own feet in surprise. In the few seconds that it took her to recover, the man had already covered several metres. She ran after him.

'You *are* John Raven – er, I mean, Maurice Harty,' she said, peering into his face. 'It is you. I watch your programme every week. I think you're brilliant!'

'I don't know who you think I am,' said the man, increasing his stride. 'But I can assure you, I don't have the slightest notion what you're talking about.'

16

Miranda grinned. 'It's OK,' she said. 'I can keep a secret. Look, I don't mean to disturb you, I mean, it must be a bit irritating to have complete strangers coming up to you and asking for your autograph and all that.' Privately Miranda thought the absolute opposite. She'd have loved to have people mobbing her everywhere she went. 'But you can't kid me – you're Maurice Harty.'

'For the last time,' snapped the man, 'my name is not Maurice Harty. And I am not an actor. I've never even heard of John Raven *or Spyglass*. Now will you please leave me alone!'

'Oh!' Miranda came to a startled halt. She stared at the man's back for a few moments as he headed into the thick patch of bushes and trees.

'What happened?' Holly asked as she and Peter came running up to Miranda.

'You didn't say anything to upset him, did you?' Peter asked anxiously.

'I hardly said a word,' said Miranda. 'I just said, you're Maurice Harty, aren't you? And he said he wasn't.'

'Oh, crumbs,' said Holly. 'How embarrassing. He looks just like him.'

'Wait a minute!' Miranda said as a little light bulb lit up inside her head. 'He said: "I've never heard of John Raven or *Spyglass*." But I never mentioned *Spyglass*. I only mentioned John Raven's name.'

'So?' asked Peter. 'If he hasn't heard of John Raven, then of *course* he won't have heard of *Spyglass*. I'd have thought that's pretty obvious, even to you.'

'Dimwit!' said Miranda. 'If he's never heard of *Spyglass*, how does he know what it's called? I didn't tell him.'

'He must have denied it to avoid being pestered,' said Holly. 'I can understand that.'

'But we're his number one fans,' said Miranda. 'What on earth is the point of going to all the bother of being a famous actor if you don't like fans coming up to you?'

'I've got an idea,' said Peter. 'Let's do what Holly suggested: follow him to where he lives and then write him a really, really polite letter. He might not like being approached in the street, but he can't object to being sent a fan letter, surely?'

'We'd better get our skates on, then,' said Miranda. 'He's already out of sight. Once he leaves the park, there's four or five ways he could go.'

'OK,' said Holly. 'Operation Follow John Raven. Keep quiet, and keep well back.'

They walked briskly along the path and into the dense patch of trees and rhodo-dendron bushes. The path did a couple of wiggles and shakes. Two small children came running along, followed by a tired-looking woman with a pushchair.

'We'd better speed up,' said Peter. 'We'll lose him otherwise.'

They trotted past an old disused drinking fountain and came to a clear stretch of path. Ahead of them they could see past the trees and into the open grass. There were the iron railings that surrounded the park, and the wrought-iron gates standing open. But there was no sign of Maurice Harty. Not even a distant glimpse of his raincoated back leaving the park.

'That's weird,' said Holly. 'He must have run like a maniac.'

'He'd have to be some sort of Olympic

19

sprinter to have got right across there and out of sight,' said Peter.

'So where's he vanished to?' asked Miranda.

'He must have gone off the path,' said Holly. 'Perhaps he realised we were following him and dived into cover.' Her eyes gleamed. 'That's just the sort of thing John Raven would do if he was being followed. He'd duck behind a tree and then come up behind them with his gun.'

The three of them glanced nervously behind them. The path was empty.

'Look,' said Peter, 'if he's that anxious to avoid handing out autographs, maybe we should just forget about it.'

'No way!' said Miranda. 'I'm going to find him.'

'But . . .' Peter began.

'Don't worry,' said Miranda. 'I'm not going to do a rugby tackle on him and sit on his head until he admits who he is. We want his address, don't we? And that means finding him again and sneakily following him home.'

'If he is avoiding us,' said Holly, 'then he's probably just taken a detour through the trees. He might go out through the entrance down there.' She pointed to the left. There were four ways in and out of the park, one at each corner. Maurice and the Mystery Kids had been heading for the gate at the northwestern side. Holly's idea was that he may be heading for the gate at the *south*west side.

The two girls stepped off the path, pushing their way between thick bushes and coming into the trees. Peter followed them.

'This is just like an episode of *Spyglass*,' Miranda said with a grin.

'I hope not,' said Peter. 'People who follow John Raven end up either flat on their backs with bullet holes in them, or locked up in prison.'

'He won't get me,' said Miranda, crouching and holding her hands together, arms stretched out in front of her like an armed police officer.

'*Pakowee!*' she said. 'One-shot Hayes does it again. Right between the eyes.'

'I see,' Peter said dryly. 'Shoot first and ask for autographs afterwards, huh?'

'Shh!' hissed Holly. 'Look!'

21

Through the trees they could see the grey of a raincoat and a smooth sweep of black hair.

'It's him,' whispered Miranda. 'What's he doing?'

The three friends sought the cover of a thick tree. Holly peeped around the gnarled trunk.

'He's just standing there,' she said. She jerked her head back. 'He's looking round.'

Miranda knelt down in the grass and peered round the foot of the trunk, her head right down close to the ground.

'I don't believe it,' she whispered. 'I do not believe it!'

Maurice Harty was standing by an oak tree, staring around him as if scared that he was being watched. Then he opened his coat and pulled out a thick brown envelope. And even as Miranda tried to work out what on earth he was up to, he thrust the envelope into the crook of the tree, pulled his coat closed and scuttled off like a frightened rabbit.

'What?' whispered Peter.

Miranda stood up. 'You're not going to believe what I just saw,' she said.

'Yes, we will,' said Holly. 'What did you see?'

'He took a big envelope out of his coat and shoved it up the tree,' said Miranda. 'And then he ran off.'

'I don't believe it,' said Holly.

'I told you you wouldn't,' said Miranda.

'Ignore her,' said Peter. 'It's a wind-up.'

'Oh, yeah?' declared Miranda. 'We'll see about that!' She marched out from their hiding place and headed for the tree.

'She is kidding, isn't she?' Peter said to Holly.

'There's one way to find out,' said Holly.

They followed her. One part of her story was true: there was certainly no sign of Maurice Harty nearby.

'Come on,' said Miranda, standing under the tree. She pointed to the place about two metres in the air where the trunk split into two thick branches. 'In there!'

Holly reached up through the leaves. She didn't quite know what to expect, and the sensible part of her brain was telling her that this was just one of Miranda's jokes. But

23

then her groping fingers touched something smooth and flat.

'Oh!' She took hold and pulled it down from its secret nest in the tree.

'Is that or is that not a big envelope?' asked Miranda.

'It is,' Peter said in amazement. The envelope was about thirty centimetres by twenty centimetres, and very fat in the middle. He took the envelope from Holly and felt all over it, trying to guess what on earth could be inside.

'What do you think is in it?' asked Miranda. She gave the top of the envelope a prod. 'It's not sealed down very well,' she said. 'If you were to accidentally do this,' she flicked her finger in under the flap and gave a twist, 'it might sort of accidentally come open. Oops! Just like that!'

The flap lifted and the mouth of the envelope gaped. Holly leaned over Peter's shoulder as all three of them tried to see what was inside.

Peter pushed his hand in and brought the bundle out. It was a thick wad of twenty pound notes.

'There must be hundreds of pounds here!' gasped Miranda as the three of them stared at the money in amazement. 'Why would *anyone* leave an envelope full of cash up a tree?'

**Elementary**

Miranda looked round, her eyes narrowed suspiciously.

'OK,' she said loudly, 'you can come out now, I'm on to you!'

Peter and Holly stared at her.

'Don't you get it?' said Miranda. 'This is a set up. We've walked right into one of those television programmes where they secretly film people making complete twerps of themselves. There'll be someone hiding nearby with a camera.'

'I don't think so,' said Holly.

The three of them stared into the trees.

'Do you see anyone?' asked Peter.

'Nope,' said Holly.

'Oh!' said Miranda. 'Maybe it isn't that, then. Maybe they're filming a location shot scene for *Spyglass* and we've walked straight into it!'

'There'd still be cameras,' Peter pointed out. 'And by now there'd be a pretty annoyed director heading in our direction.'

'He's right, you know,' said Holly. 'Whatever's going on here, it's not being filmed.'

'So why did Maurice Harty shove all that money in a tree?' asked Miranda. She looked from Holly to Peter and back to Holly again. 'Well? Any ideas?'

'I'll tell you my favourite idea,' said Peter. 'How about we put the envelope back where we found it and get out of here as fast as we can?'

'For crying out loud,' said Miranda. 'Of all the weedy—'

'Shh!' hissed Holly. 'Someone's coming!'

They followed the line of her gaze. A yellow shape was moving through the bushes near the path.

'Put it back,' Peter said, pushing the money back into the envelope and thrusting it into Holly's hands.

Holly dropped the envelope as if it was red hot.

'I don't want it,' she said.

Miranda stooped and picked it up.

27

'Put it back where we found it,' Peter said in near-panic. 'Let's get out of here!'

The approaching yellow shape could now be seen to be a coat. In a flurry of arms and legs, the three Mystery Kids dashed for cover. They dived behind a large stretch of bushes and lay perfectly still on the ground, their hearts beating like hammers.

'Did he see us?' Peter moaned.

'I don't think so,' said Holly. She lifted her head and crawled along until she could see the tree. 'It's not a *he*,' she said. 'It's a *she*.'

Holly could see the person in the yellow coat quite clearly. It was a woman. She was wearing a headscarf, facing away from them as she lifted an arm and groped in the crook of the tree.

'She's going for the envelope,' whispered Holly.

'Uh-oh,' said Miranda.

'Has she got it?' asked Peter.

'No,' said Holly. 'Her hand's come out empty. She's looking round. She's feeling up there with both hands now. For heaven's sake, Miranda, where did you put it?'

'Here,' Miranda said sheepishly. Miranda had the thick envelope in her hand.

'Nice one, Miranda,' said Peter.

'She's looking at her watch, I think,' Holly said as she peered under the bush. 'Now she's walking away. She's heading back to the path. She's gone.' Holly pushed herself out from under the bush and sat up. She brushed earth and twigs and bits of leaf off her front.

'I've got a horrible feeling I know what's going on here,' said Peter.

'Never mind your horrible feelings,' said Miranda. 'I'll tell you what all this is about. Maurice Harty is being blackmailed!'

'I was going to say that,' said Peter. 'That's *exactly* what I was just about to say!'

'Blackmailed?' breathed Holly. 'Never! I don't believe it.'

'What else could it be?' asked Miranda.

'Maybe they were *rehearsing*,' said Holly. 'You know, rehearsing a scene out of a new episode of *Spyglass*.'

Peter looked at her. 'You don't really believe that, do you? They were never rehearsing. Not in a million years.'

'I suppose not.' Holly looked uneasily at her two friends. 'I think we'd better get back to our office and have a good think about this,' she said.

'What about the money?' asked Miranda. 'Shall I put it back up the tree?'

'I don't think there'd be any point,' said Peter. 'They must have arranged a particular time for him to leave the money. The woman will just assume he never put it there.'

'Oh, wow,' breathed Miranda. 'We might have got him into some bad trouble.'

'What do you mean, *we*?' said Peter. '*You* ran off with the envelope. I said to put it back.'

'Never mind about that,' said Holly. 'Whatever's going on with this money, we've messed it all up.' She looked determinedly at her two friends. 'So *we've* got to come up with some way of putting things right.'

The three of them were back in their office in Peter's house. Holly was sitting at the desk, counting through the bundle of twenty pound notes for the third time.

Miranda and Peter were watching her;

Miranda perched up on the windowsill and Peter sitting on the corner of the desk.

'One thousand nine hundred and eighty,' Holly said. She placed the last note on top of the others. 'Two thousand!'

'Oh, wow,' said Miranda. 'Two thousand pounds. I've never seen two thousand pounds before.'

'I wish I hadn't seen *this* two thousand pounds,' said Peter. 'What on earth are we going to do with it?'

'We could take it straight to the police,' said Holly. 'Tell them the whole story.'

'But what if we're right and he *is* being blackmailed?' said Miranda. 'If we tell the police, they'll want to investigate. Maurice Harty could end up in real trouble. It would get in the newspapers and everything. And then the people who make *Spyglass* would find out, and he'd get sacked and there'd be no more episodes of *Spyglass*. And it'd all be our fault!' Miranda looked anxiously at the other two. 'Do we really want to be responsible for having *Spyglass* taken off TV?'

Her two friends stared at her in silence

for a few moments. She blinked breathlessly at them.

'Well?' she said. '*Do* we?'

Holly shook her head.

'OK, then,' said Peter. 'We put the money back and hope for the best.'

'There's no point in doing that,' said Holly. 'The woman came and went. What we've got to do is get the money back to Maurice Harty somehow.' She patted the notes into a neat pile and pushed them back into the envelope. 'We can write him an anonymous letter,' she said. She opened a drawer and took out a note pad. 'Dear Mr Harty,' she said as she wrote. 'We saw you put this in a tree in Belair Park. We didn't realise what it was. Sorry. Some friends.' She sucked the end of her pen as she re-read her note. 'P.S.' she continued. 'The woman came to pick it up but we'd already taken it. Sorry again.'

She looked at the others. 'What do you think?'

'Fine,' said Peter. 'There's just one tiny problem. We don't know where he lives.'

'Ah,' Holly said, waving her pen in the air in the way that she had seen John Raven do

32

just before explaining a bit of clever detection. 'But we *do*!'

'We do?' said Miranda. 'How?'

'Elementary, my dear Miranda,' said Holly. 'It's been staring us in the face all the time.' She pointed the pen at the photograph of Maurice Harty and his family pinned to their noticeboard.

Peter and Miranda looked at the photo.

'Excuse me if I'm being dim,' said Peter. 'But I think I'd have remembered if they'd mentioned his address. All we know is that he lives in Highgate. What are we going to do? Knock on every door in every street around here until we find him?'

'I excuse you for being dim,' said Holly. '*Look* at the picture.'

They all looked. Maurice Harty and his wife and daughter sat, as ever, on the sofa in a back room. Behind them the French windows opened on to a garden.

Holly leaned over the desk and tapped the picture with the end of her pen.

'What's that in the background?' she said.

'A church spire,' said Miranda.

'Hold on,' Peter said, looking more closely.

'There's a weather vane on the top of the spire. I can't quite make it out. It's pretty blurry.'

'I think you'll find it's an angel blowing a trumpet,' said Holly. Now that she pointed it out, both Miranda and Peter could see that the vague shape on the spire could easily be an angel, lying down on its front and holding a trumpet to its mouth. 'And the only church around here with that on its spire is Saint Jude's,' said Holly.

'And the church is right at the end of their garden,' said Peter. 'So they must live in a street that backs on to the church! Holly, you're a genius!'

'I haven't finished yet,' said Holly, modestly trying to disguise a triumphant smile. 'Look at the sky.'

'OK,' said Miranda. 'I'm looking. It's all kind of orangey and reddy, like a sunset. Oh! I get it! Sunset!'

'The sun sets in the west,' Peter interrupted. 'Which means the road that Maurice Harty lives in must be due *east* of Saint Jude's, because we can see the sun setting behind the church.'

Holly jumped up and went over to their wall map. It only took her a few seconds to locate Saint Jude's church.

'Benedict Avenue!' she said. 'Look. It must be!' Her finger traced a curved road that ran north-south on the right hand side of the church. 'Maurice Harty lives in that road! You can bank on it!'

'And there's all that tall pampas grass in his garden,' said Peter, glancing back at the photo. 'So all we've got to do is find the house with the pampas grass, and we've done it.'

'So, what are we waiting for?' asked Miranda. 'Let's go!'

'One last thing,' said Holly. She leaned over the note. 'P.P.S.,' she said as she wrote. 'We really like you in *Spyglass*.'

She looked up at her friends. 'There we are,' she said as she tucked the note into the bulging envelope. She took out a roll of tape and stuck the flap down. 'Now all we've got to do is push this through his letter-box without being seen.'

'Disguises!' yelled Miranda.

'No!' Holly said firmly. 'No disguises. We just get rid of this money and get away from there as quickly as we can. Agreed?'

Peter and Miranda nodded and the three friends went running down the stairs and out of the house.

Holly couldn't help the sinking feeling in her stomach that hit her every time she thought about Maurice Harty being black-mailed.

What could he possibly have done? It was obviously something he wanted kept quiet. Holly just hoped that they were doing the right thing in not going straight to the police. She just hoped Maurice Harty wasn't involved in anything criminal.

**Money trouble**

'See anything?' asked Miranda.

'Keep your voice down!' Holly whispered as she clutched the top of the door to the side alley and lifted her eyes over the edge. Peter winced as Holly's shoes dug into his cupped hands.

The three friends were in Benedict Avenue, a long, tree-lined crescent of semi-detached Victorian houses with deep front gardens and an air of quiet serenity.

They had to find the rear garden with the tall sprays of pampas grass. Which was why the three of them had crept into the first front garden and why Holly had got Peter to give her a boost up so that she could see over the side door.

'Be quick!' said Peter. 'Someone could come along at any minute!'

'Oh, pooh!' said Miranda. 'I'm keeping watch, aren't I? I'll spot anyone coming before they – *ooh*! Ah! Er – hello.'

'What are you doing in here?' An elderly man had come around the bay window and was staring at the Mystery Kids with an angry look on his face.

'It's not what you think,' said Holly, trying to turn in Peter's hands. She lost her grip and the two of them came crashing to the ground.

'We're, er . . . we're doing a survey,' stammered Miranda while Peter and Holly picked themselves up.

'A survey?' said the man. 'What survey? What are you talking about?'

Miranda's mouth opened and closed a couple of times, making her look a bit like a startled fish.

'We're doing a survey for our school on pampas grass,' said Miranda. 'We have to find out how many people have pampas grass in their gardens. Do you have pampas grass in your back garden?'

'No, I don't,' said the man. He looked totally baffled. 'And I'm sure your teachers didn't intend for you to trespass on people's property.' His eyebrows lowered suspiciously. 'What school do you go to?'

'You see!' Holly said to Miranda. 'I told you this wasn't the way to do it!' She gave the old man an apologetic smile. 'I'm really sorry that we bothered you.' She frowned at Miranda. 'Didn't I say all along that we should ring people's doorbells first?'

'I think we'd better go,' said Peter, giving the old man what he hoped looked like an innocent smile.

'Wait a minute,' said the man as the three friends sidled past him. 'I want to know what school you go to.'

'The John Raven School,' said Holly as they edged to the gate.

'We're really sorry to have bothered you,' said Peter as they exited through the front gate.

'We'll put you down as no pampas grass,' added Miranda. 'Thanks for your help.'

'Now just wait a minute!' called the old man. 'I've never heard of the John Raven School.'

The three friends didn't wait a minute. They didn't even wait a second. They ran!

Three heads peered round the corner into Benedict Avenue. The old man hadn't come out on to the pavement.

'A survey of pampas grass!' said Peter. 'Good grief!'

'I didn't notice you coming up with anything better,' said Miranda. She grinned at Holly. 'I liked that bit about the John Raven School.'

'Do you think he's gone indoors?' asked Holly. 'I can't see.'

'Even if he has gone inside, you can bet he'll be keeping watch through the window,' said Peter. 'There's no way I'm trying that again. We'll have to think of something else.'

'What other way is there?' asked Miranda. 'We've got to be able to see over the side doors in order to get a look at the back gardens. How else are we going to do it? Attach powerful springs to our shoes and bounce down the road looking over the rooftops?'

Holly stepped into the open. Peter was right. They couldn't risk getting caught again. But what else was there to do?

A red hatchback car drove past them along

the road. It slowed and pulled into the kerb about a third of the way along.

'Well?' asked Miranda. 'What's our brilliant new plan, then?'

Holly shrugged.

'I don't know,' she sighed.

Peter was gazing past her shoulder. The red car had stopped. A woman got out. She was somewhere in her late teens with a huge mass of golden brown hair and a red dress that seemed several sizes too tight for her. But it wasn't the woman who was holding Peter's attention; it was the girl who got out of the car with her. A girl he recognised.

'Don't look round,' whispered Peter.

Both Miranda and Holly instantly looked round.

'What?' asked Holly. 'Oh!' She recognised the thin, blonde-haired girl as well. It was Bethany Harty, Maurice's daughter.

The woman took the girl's hand and pulled her into the front garden of one of the houses. Judging by the way the little girl dragged her feet, Holly was pretty sure the two of them didn't get on very well.

41

And the young woman definitely wasn't Maurice Harty's wife, Holly was sure of that.

'Why do you always do that?' asked Peter. 'I say "don't look round," and the first thing you do is look round!'

'Listen, Peter,' said Holly. 'If you don't want someone to look round, then the *last* thing you say to them is "don't look round". There isn't a single person in the whole world who wouldn't look round if they're told not to.' She made a mental note of the house into which the woman and the girl had gone. 'Anyway,' she said, 'now we know where Maurice and his family live.'

'So let's get rid of this envelope,' said Miranda. The big envelope was tucked down her jeans under her red pullover.

'Uh-oh!' said Peter. 'Eyeball alert!'

'What?' asked Miranda.

'We're being watched,' hissed Peter. He cocked his head to where they could see the old man peering at them from round the edge of his privet hedge.

'We'd better disappear,' said Holly. 'He's

suspicious enough as it is. We don't want him ending up phoning the police about us.'

'So what do we do about the envelope?' asked Miranda.

'We hang on to it,' said Holly. 'And we post it through Maurice Harty's door on our way home from school tomorrow. We can't do anything else today, not with that man peering at us.'

'So one of us has to look after two thousand pounds all tonight and all through tomorrow?' said Miranda. 'Well, good luck to whoever does it!'

'I think Miranda should look after it,' said Peter.

'*I* should?' shrieked Miranda.

'Well volunteered,' said Holly. 'Don't worry, Miranda. All you have to do is sleep with it under your pillow tonight, and then shove it right down at the bottom of your bag at school tomorrow.'

'Yes, but, what if—'

'Stop panicking!' Peter interrupted her. 'Nothing's going to happen.' He looked closely at her. 'You're not scared are you?'

'No!' Miranda said automatically. 'I'm not scared of anything!'

Holly grinned. 'So what's the problem?' she asked.

Miranda let out a deep sigh. 'There's no problem,' she said. 'You two just leave all the really difficult stuff to me. As usual!'

'Good,' said Holly. 'That's agreed, then.'

And that was what happened. Miranda ended up in charge of the alarming envelope. And she did put it under her pillow that night, although she didn't sleep very well.

If a burglar or blackmailer, or anyone else for that matter, had come within five metres of Miranda's bed that night, they'd have been bashed with a pillow and deafened by the loudest scream Miranda could have managed.

'I'll be home late from school!' Holly called as she grabbed her jacket and bag and ran for the front door.

Her mother's head appeared round the kitchen door. 'Where will you be?' she asked.

'I'll give you two guesses,' said Mr Adams. He came out of the kitchen in his blue suit. He was a successful and hard-working solicitor, although his real joy was carpentry. The cellar of their house was filled with his tools, and he spent every spare moment down there, making the most beautiful wooden furniture Holly had ever seen.

'She'll be at Peter's house or at Miranda's house.' He grinned at Holly. 'Am I right?'

'Probably Peter's house,' said Holly.

'Ring us if you're going to be later than usual,' said Mrs Adams. There was a thunder of feet down the stairs and Holly was nearly knocked flying as a small whirlwind went careering along the hall to the front door. Jamie, Holly's little brother.

'Have you remembered your lunch?' Mrs Adams called after Jamie.

'Sinmebag,' gabbled Jamie as he tore the door open and ran out into the street. 'Castopnowbuscomin'.'

'I think maybe he's late for the bus,' said Mr Adams with a grin.

'I called him three times,' sighed Mrs Adams. She looked at Holly. 'I'll be glad

45

when he's old enough to go to secondary school. At least you'll be able to keep an eye on him then.'

'Thanks very much,' said Holly. The idea didn't appeal to her at all. She'd done enough Jamie-watching at primary school. She wasn't looking forward to starting all over again.

Holly met up with Peter and Miranda. Miranda was in a bad way.

'I hardly got a wink of sleep all night,' she complained. 'I kept thinking some burglar was going to sneak in and whip the envelope out from under my pillow. You two don't realise how worrying it is.'

'Don't fret about it,' said Holly. 'We'll keep close to you, and in a few hours we'll be rid of it, OK?'

'A few hours,' groaned Miranda. 'I'll be a nervous wreck in a few hours!'

They approached Benedict Avenue from the other end. The last thing they wanted to risk was being spotted by that old man again. Miranda had the envelope hidden in her school bag. It felt like a huge, shining beacon to every villain and criminal in the whole of London, and Miranda was very worried about it.

'Look,' Peter said, trying to reassure her. 'No one knows you've got all that money on you. It's perfectly safe.'

'If it's so safe, how come I got lumbered with it?' asked Miranda. 'I notice you two were quick enough to volunteer me to look after it.'

'Only because we knew you'd be best at it,' said Holly. 'Now, try to look perfectly ordinary and normal, as if we walk home from school this way every day. Miranda! Stop whistling! Why do you always start whistling when you're trying not to be noticed?'

'Sorry,' said Miranda. 'I didn't know I did.'

'Well, you do,' said Peter.

They approached the house into which the woman and the little girl had gone the previous afternoon.

'Go on, then,' said Holly, giving Miranda a nudge. 'Bung it through the letter-box and let's get out of here.'

Miranda swivelled her head in all directions before starting nervously up the front path. The red hatchback car was parked at the kerb, Holly had noticed, although she didn't mention it to Miranda. There was no point in making her even more anxious.

Miranda stepped into the porch and pulled the envelope out of her bag. She looked uneasily at it and then at the letter-box. Large envelope, small letter-box.

She glanced round at her two friends. Holly gave her a look to urge her to hurry. Peter was watching up and down the avenue.

Miranda did her best to cram the envelope through the letter-box. She tried folding it in half, but the thick wad of money inside wouldn't fold properly and the result was a doubled-over envelope that was almost thicker than it was wide.

Then she tried folding in the edges of the envelope.

'Hah!' She was able to ease the end of the envelope in through the letter-box. It didn't help that she was beginning to get into a bit of a panic that she'd be caught.

The reluctant envelope edged forwards centimetre by centimetre as Miranda sawed it to and fro and pushed with both hands.

'*Yowww!*' she yelled as the envelope suddenly whipped forwards, dragging her hands in with it and causing the letter-box flap to snap down on her fingers. 'Ow! Yow-ow-ow!'

'Miranda!' Holly couldn't understand why her friend had suddenly started yelling and dancing about in the porch.

Before Miranda was able to extract her trapped fingers, the front door of the house opened from the inside. Miranda was towed over the threshold. She tripped and fell to her knees, both hands caught firmly by the letter-box flap.

She found herself looking up into a pair of inquisitive blue eyes.

'My dad isn't in,' said the girl. 'My name's Bethany. What are you doing?'

**Creepy Crawly**

Bethany's bright eyes sparkled with amuse-
ment as she looked down at Miranda, kneeling on her doormat and trapped by both
hands through the letter-box.

'I was just delivering a parcel,' groaned
Miranda. 'Can you get me out of this?'

'Of course.' Bethany pushed the letter-box
flap up. Miranda gave a yelp as her fingers
came free.

Holly and Peter came running up the path.
Holly saw that the girl was holding the
envelope in her hand. Miranda was kneeling
halfway through the open doorway, shaking
her fingers and blowing on them.

'Hello,' Bethany said coolly. 'Who are you?'

'We're just – um, fans,' Holly said as she
hauled Miranda to her feet. 'Fans of your
father.'

'Oh, some of *those*,' Bethany said in a world-weary manner. She looked at the envelope. 'Is this thing a fan letter?'

'Yes,' said Holly.

'No,' said Peter at the same time.

They looked at each other.

'No,' said Holly.

'Yes,' said Peter.

'For heaven's sake!' said Miranda. She smiled at Bethany. 'I'm sorry about my friends. It's a sort of fan letter, but not really,' she explained to Bethany. 'Can you just give it to your father when he gets home? It's quite important.'

Much to the horror of the three friends, Bethany shoved a finger under the sealed-down flap and tore it open.

'No!' yelled Holly. 'Don't!'

'It's OK,' said Bethany. 'I deal with all my dad's fan mail. Do you want a signed photo? If you want to . . .' Her voice trailed off as she looked into the envelope.

She blinked a couple of times, as if she thought her eyes were playing tricks on her.

'Your dad dropped it,' began Holly. 'In the

park. Belair Park.' She hooked a thumb over her shoulder. 'Back there.'

'I know where Belair Park is,' said Bethany. She looked at the three friends with uncomfortably bright eyes. 'Dad dropped this in Belair Park?'

'That's right,' said Peter.

'When?'

'He dropped it yesterday,' said Holly.

'You saw him drop it?' asked Bethany.

'That's right,' said Peter, nodding encouragingly at the young girl. 'It fell out of his pocket, so we thought we'd better give it back. That's why we're here.' He gave her what he hoped looked like the sort of smile you give to little children.

Bethany gave him a hollow look, as if she thought he was a bit silly. 'So why didn't you give it back to him at the time?' she asked.

'Ah,' said Holly. 'Good question.'

Bethany gave them a worried frown. 'What's Dad been up to?' she asked. 'He's been acting strangely for weeks now.'

'Can we trust you?' Holly asked Bethany.

'Of course,' said Bethany.

'You see,' Holly began hesitantly. Then she

paused. Bethany was clearly intelligent and on the ball, but was it really a good idea to tell her how they'd come by the money? And could they really tell her that they believed that her father was being blackmailed?

'Bethany!' It was a woman's voice, calling up from the back of the house. 'What are you doing?'

'Don't say anything,' whispered Bethany. 'Not a word!'

Holly and the others stared at her in bafflement as she crammed the envelope up her sweat-shirt.

The golden-haired woman appeared, frowning. Her heels clicked on the stripped pine floorboards as she stalked along the hall.

'What's going on?' she asked. She looked icily at the three friends.

*Too much lipstick*, Holly thought as she looked at the woman's huge, pillar-box red mouth. *Too much makeup altogether*.

'Who are these children?' snapped the woman.

'Friends of mine,' said Bethany.

The woman's eyes narrowed suspiciously. 'I haven't seen them before.'

'You don't know all my friends, Claire,' said Bethany. 'It's OK. They're fans of my father.'

Claire gave the three of them a final, paint-peeling stare.

'Make sure you close the door properly,' she said as she turned on her heel. 'And don't make a mess.'

Holly saw Bethany stick her tongue out at Claire's back as the young woman disppeared back down the hall and round a corner.

'Isn't she the most horrible person you've ever met?' Bethany said once the woman was out of earshot. She giggled. 'Her last name's Crawley. Claire Crawley. I call her Creepy Crawly. She's our au pair. Do you want to see my dad's study?' This last comment was so unexpected that it was a moment or two before it sank in.

'Do you think he'd mind?' asked Peter.

'No way,' said Bethany. 'No problem.' She looked keenly at the three friends. 'But you've got to tell me the truth about this money,' she said, patting the bulging front of her sweat-shirt.

'Deal,' said Miranda, her eyes like saucers

as she gazed round the hall. It was very elegant, all stripped pine with throw rugs on the floor and watercolour prints on the ivory-white walls. There was a cabinet against one wall and one of those tall wooden coat stands with long, curling hooks at the top.

'Come on, then,' said Bethany. 'I'll show you the *sanctum sanctorum*.'

'The what?' asked Holly.

'Dad's study,' explained Bethany. 'He calls it his *sanctum sanctorum*. Don't ask me what that means.' She led them a little way along the hall to a natural-wood door.

They stepped over the threshold and found themselves in the very room from the Sunday newspaper supplement photograph.

'Ohh . . .' Holly breathed, gazing round in awe. 'Oh, wow.' She could hardly believe it. They were actually in Maurice Harty's house. In his study. In the study where he probably learned the very lines that they heard every week coming out of the mouth of Secret Agent John Raven!

There was a huge desk covered in books, magazines, papers and other important-looking things. He even had one of those old-fashioned telephones; the big black ones that Holly only ever saw in old black-and-white movies on TV.

There was the leather sofa on which the Harty family had been sitting when they had their photo taken. And behind it, through the closed French windows, Holly saw the tall sprays of pampas grass and the spire of Saint Jude's church.

The walls were filled with bookcases and glass-fronted display cases, and the only remaining sections of wall were hung with film posters and photographs of Maurice Harty with various celebrities.

'I can't believe it,' breathed Miranda. 'We're actually in John Raven's study. I can't believe it!'

Bethany grinned at them.

'You *are* big fans, aren't you?' she said.

'You'd better believe it,' breathed Miranda. 'The biggest!'

Peter walked soft-footed over to one of the display cabinets. It was filled with rank after rank of model soldiers. Hundreds of them. Some in red tunics with tall, black busbys and long rifles over their shoulders. Some in blue tunics with plumes in their hats, marching eternally forwards with fixed bayonets. Some on horseback with gleaming swords in their exquisitely painted hands.

'All these toy soldiers,' said Peter in amazement. 'He must have hundreds of them.'

'Thousands,' said Bethany. 'But you'd better not let him hear you calling them toys. They're models.'

'What's the difference?' asked Miranda as she wandered round the long room, almost in a daze.

'A few hundred pounds for a start,' said Bethany. She walked over to where Peter was standing. 'See that one?' She pointed at a rather magnificent soldier on a black horse.

'That's Arthur Wellesley,' she said. 'He cost dad two hundred and fifty pounds.'

'Oh,' said Peter. 'Arthur Wellesley, huh?'

Bethany gave him a long look. 'You don't know who Arthur Wellesley was, do you?' she said. 'Lord Wellington! The guy who beat Napoleon. I suppose you've heard of Napoleon?'

'Of course I have,' said Peter, slightly put out by being made to look dim by a girl five years younger than himself. 'He was French, wasn't he?'

'Corsican, actually,' said Bethany with a smile. 'But you're close enough.' She turned to Holly. 'Now, are you going to tell me about this money?'

Holly was about to speak when Bethany made a shushing motion and ran over to the study door. She listened for a few seconds.

'It's OK,' she said. 'We can talk. I was just checking that Creepy wasn't hanging around. I always get the feeling with her that everything I say is being listened to. And she's always watching me. And I don't mean watching *out* for me. I mean watching me in a nasty way. Like cats watch mice.'

'Why don't you ask your dad to find another au pair?' asked Miranda. 'If she's that bad.'

'Dad's got enough on his mind right now,' said Bethany. 'My mum's away filming in America for three months, and I'm sure Dad's not well.' She shook her head, her eyes filling with sudden sadness. 'Tell me all about this

58

money,' she said, her face determined. 'I want to know the truth.'

Falteringly, Holly told her exactly what they had seen in the park the previous afternoon.

In the silence that followed, Bethany looked thoughtfully at the three of them. 'I see,' she said. 'And you think Dad's being blackmailed by this woman?'

'Of course not,' said Peter. 'That never crossed our minds, did it, Holly? Did it, Miranda?'

'I'm not thick,' said Bethany. 'And neither are you. But if you're going to carry on pretending to be thick, we're not going to get anywhere.' She looked straight into Holly's eyes. 'I've got to try and help him,' she said. 'If you agree to help me, I'll tell you some more stuff.'

'We'll do anything we can,' said Miranda. 'We're his number one fans.'

'Do you know what this is all about?' asked Peter. '*Is* your dad being blackmailed?'

'I know there's something wrong with him,' said Bethany. 'He's having blackouts. He's been trying to hide it from me, but I came down here late one night last week and I found him lying on the floor, over there.' She pointed to a large persian rug stretched on the floor in the front part of the long room. 'He was fully dressed and he had his coat on, as if he'd just come home, but he hadn't been out all evening. Then Creepy Crawly came in and she said she'd look after him. She sent me off to bed.'

'Did she call a doctor?' asked Holly.

'No, I don't think so,' said Bethany. 'I came down the next morning to see how Dad was. He was in here, still in the same clothes, sitting at the desk and staring at a model soldier.' Bethany moved round the desk and sat in the large leather armchair. She leaned forwards, her face taking on a curious expression; half shock, half disbelief, staring at an imaginary something that Holly guessed must have been standing on the green blotter.

'That's how he looked,' said Bethany. 'Still in his coat and everything, just staring at this soldier. A drummer boy in a Napoleonic uniform. I've never seen it before. It was painted gold. But as soon as he saw me, he grabbed it and shoved it in his coat pocket.'

'So what did he do then?' asked Miranda.

'He told me to go and get ready for school,' said Bethany. 'I asked him what was wrong, but he said he was just tired.' Bethany looked anxiously at the three friends. 'He was tired, but there was something else, something in the way he was behaving that really upset me. It was like he was shutting me out of something. As if there was something going on that he didn't want me to know about.

'That evening, when I asked him about the golden drummer boy, he told me he'd sold it.' Bethany frowned. 'But he never sells any of his models, not unless he's got a duplicate. And he certainly doesn't have another golden drummer boy.' Her eyes filled with anxious tears. 'And I think there's something really wrong with him, but he won't tell me. And now there's this money!' She pulled the envelope out from inside her sweat-shirt and let the bundle of twenty pound notes fall to the floor.

Holly stepped forwards to comfort the distressed girl.

A sudden sound from the door made them all look round. The door burst open and Claire came marching into the room.

'What are you doing in here?' she demanded.

# Something nasty in the post

'Don't shout at me!' Bethany said to the young woman. 'I'm allowed to come in here whenever I like.'

Claire's eyes raked over the three friends, as if she suspected them all of having stuffed their pockets with Maurice Harty's precious model soldiers.

But it wasn't that which alarmed Holly. It was the bundle of notes which lay openly at Bethany's feet. Claire only had to glance down and she'd see it.

Holly acted as quick as lightning. She gave the bundle as swift kick with her heel so that it went shooting under the desk, and then she grabbed Bethany by the shoulders and turned her away from the door so that Claire wouldn't be able to see that the girl was almost in tears.

63

'Hold still,' said Holly. 'Look up. I think I see it.'

Miranda caught on immediately. 'Bethany's got something in her eye,' she said to Claire. 'It's probably only an eyelash.'

'There!' said Holly, pretending to sweep something out of Bethany's eye. 'That's got it.'

Holly had the uncomfortable feeling that the scarlet-lipped young woman had been listening at the door. If Bethany didn't like or trust her, then Holly was determined that Claire Crawley wasn't going to find out anything about the money that they had found.

Bethany turned, rubbing her eye. 'Did you want something, Claire?' she asked.

'I only wanted to know what you'd like for your tea,' said Claire.

'Hamburgers, please,' said Bethany.

'We don't have any hamburgers,' said Claire.

'OK, pizza.'

'You had the last of the pizza yesterday,' said Claire.

Bethany frowned at her. 'So what have we got?' she asked.

64

'Fish fingers,' said Claire.

'Fine,' said Bethany. 'I'll have fish fingers, then.' She glared at Claire. 'Thank you.'

Claire gave her a cold look and then left the room, slamming the door behind herself.

Miranda opened her mouth to speak, but Bethany waved her into silence. Bethany crept across the floor and pulled the door open with a jerk. Claire almost fell into the room, a look of shock on her face.

'Did you want something else?' Bethany asked as Claire recovered herself.

Without a word, Claire turned and went click-click-clicking down the hall.

'She was listening!' said Peter.

'I told you,' said Bethany. 'She's always listening and watching.'

'You don't think she might have something to do with your dad being blackmailed, do you?' asked Miranda.

Bethany shook her head. 'No, she's nasty, but I don't think she's that bad. Besides, she was recommended to Dad by someone who works at the studio.' She looked at the three friends. 'But that doesn't mean I want her knowing all about Dad's problems.' She

65

glared at the closed door. 'Huh! Came to ask what I wanted for tea! I *bet*! She was just listening in, like she always does.'

'I think you're probably right,' said Holly. 'About her eavesdropping on us, I mean. Why would she ask you what you want to eat when all she's got is fish fingers?'

'She might have wanted to know how you'd like them prepared,' said Miranda. 'Grilled, boiled or fried.'

'Boiled?' said Peter. 'You don't boil fish-fingers.'

'You get boiled fish,' said Miranda.

'Yeah, but not—'

'When you two have quite finished!' Holly interrupted. She looked at Bethany. 'You said you wanted us to help you. What do you want us to do?'

'Come up to my room,' said Bethany. 'It's more private up there.' She crouched down and retrieved the bundle of money from under the desk, shoving it back up her sweat-shirt.

She led them up through the tall house. The walls of the stairway were dotted with more photos and film posters and theatre

66

posters. Holly realised for the first time that Maurice Harty had had quite a long career before he'd become John Raven. If all those posters were anything to go by, he must have been in dozens and dozens of films and plays.

'What's it like having a famous father?' Miranda asked as they ascended yet another staircase.

'I don't know,' said Bethany. 'Here we are.' She led them into a large room under the eaves of the roof. The walls were painted bright yellow and there was all the clutter you would expect from a seven year old girl. Clothes and books and magazines and toys and dolls and school stuff, strewn all over the place.

'What do you mean, you don't know?' asked Miranda.

Bethany smiled at her. 'Dad's just dad,' she said. 'I can't really tell you what it's like having a famous father because I don't know what it's like *not* having a famous father. I suppose it's just totally normal to me.'

'Do you sit and watch *Spyglass* together?' asked Holly.

Bethany shook her head. 'Dad never watches himself on TV,' she said. 'He says it depresses him too much.'

'I can understand that,' said Peter. 'I suppose he sees himself and thinks how he could have done it better.'

'Not really,' said Bethany. 'He says he always looks seven pounds heavier on TV than he is in real life. It drives him crazy.'

Holly went over to the window. It overlooked the long garden and gave a perfect view of the lovely old church against the brightness of the afternoon sunlight.

'Is there anything else you want to tell us?' asked Holly.

'I don't know if it's got anything to do with the blackmail,' said Bethany. 'But I'm sure it's got something to do with Dad not being very well.' She joined Holly at the window. 'I woke up in the middle of the night the day after I'd seen Dad with the model drummer boy,' she said. 'I must have heard a noise in the garden. I was only half-awake, but I saw it. I know it wasn't a dream.'

'You saw what?' breathed Miranda.

'Dad was digging at the bottom of the garden,' said Claire.

'What time was this, did you say?' asked Peter.

'That's the whole point,' said Bethany. 'It was about three o'clock in the morning. When I asked Dad about it the next day, he just said he couldn't sleep and that he was doing a bit of gardening to pass the time.'

'Gardening at night?' Holly said thoughtfully. 'That doesn't sound very likely.'

'I really think Dad's ill,' said Bethany. 'But he won't listen to me. And he won't go to a doctor. And perhaps, I don't know, perhaps someone knows he's ill – that he's having these blackouts – and is threatening to tell the people at the studio.'

'Why should that be a problem?' asked Peter.

'Because Dad's contract is up for renewal in a couple of weeks,' said Bethany. 'What do you think the people with the money are going to say if they find out Dad's having a . . . a kind of nervous breakdown?'

'If things are really that serious,' said Holly,

'don't you think you should contact your mother? She should be here to help.'

'My mother is doing location work in the Rocky Mountains for the next month,' said Bethany. 'She can't just drop everything because I think Dad's ill. Especially when he won't admit it.'

'So what are we going to do?' asked Miranda. 'How can we help?'

'I don't know,' said Bethany. She gazed round at the three friends. 'But I'm really glad I met you. I wouldn't tell just anyone this, but I'm really scared for Dad. And if he's being blackmailed, then I'm going to do everything I can to help him.'

Holly was finally convinced that they were right to be trying to help Maurice Harty. If Bethany was right, and her father was ill, then it was despicable of someone to take advantage of that fact just to get money out of him. Holly was determined to try and do something about it.

'We'll think of a way to help,' she said, putting her arm round Bethany's drooping shoulders. 'Don't worry.' She looked at her two friends. 'We always think of something.'

70

From the depths of the house, they heard the echo of a door slamming closed.

'That'll be Dad home,' said Bethany. 'Please, don't say anything to him about this. He won't let us help if he knows we're trying to.'

'We won't breathe a word,' said Miranda. 'Trust us!'

'I do,' said Bethany. 'Come on down with me.'

Bethany led them down the stairs. Miranda hung back, wondering how Maurice Harty would react to finding *her* in his house. After all, the last time they'd met, he'd denied even being Maurice Harty.

'Dad!' shrieked Bethany, leaping almost clear down the last flight of stairs into her father's arms.

'Oof!' he gasped as he caught hold of her and gave her a big hug. 'How's my leading girl?'

'I'm fine,' said Bethany, taking her father's hand. 'I want you to meet some new friends of mine. They're huge fans of *Spyglass*. They've been dying to meet you.'

The three of them came trooping down

into the hall, Miranda still keeping herself as much out of sight as she could.

'I'm very pleased to meet you,' said Maurice Harty, taking Holly by the hand.

'Me too,' gasped Holly, her mind spinning as she shook Secret Agent John Raven by the hand. 'I mean thanks, or . . . er, I mean, I'm . . . you've, it's . . .' Her voice faded away. 'I'm Holly,' she said.

'And you are?' asked Maurice, taking Peter's hand.

'Peter Hamilton,' said Peter. 'I'm really pleased to meet you. I've got every episode of *Spyglass* on video. Every single one. And I've got them all listed on my computer. Well, it's my dad's computer, really, but he lets me use it. I've got all the shows cross-referenced alphabetically by the title, and chronologically by date, and—'

'I'm Miranda,' interrupted Miranda, pushing past Peter. She knew that unless someone interrupted him, Peter was quite capable of going on about his computer files for the next half an hour.

Maurice Harty's eyebrows knitted as he shook Miranda's hand. It was obvious that he recognised her. Miranda wasn't the sort of person anyone could forget in a hurry.

'I'm very pleased to meet you,' he said with a big smile. 'Because it gives me the opportunity to apologise for my appalling behaviour in the park yesterday.'

'It wasn't all that appalling,' said Miranda.

'It was, and I apologise unreservedly,' said Maurice Harty, still gripping her hand. 'I can only excuse myself by saying I had the most terrible headache.' He beamed round at his daughter. 'And to think you're friends of Bethany, as well. I really am most sorry.'

'Can they stay for tea?' asked Bethany.

'Of course they can,' said Maurice with an even wider smile. 'I'd be delighted.'

Holly began to think that perhaps he was overdoing the welcome a bit. It didn't feel fake exactly, but Holly did get the impression that all his enthusiasm was intended to cover something up.

'You'd better let Claire know, though,' he said. He scooped up some mail from the hall cabinet and walked through into his study.

'Great!' smiled Bethany. 'This will really

annoy her. Three extra lots of food to pre-
pare! Ha!'

Holly and her friends hung about at the
top of the stairs as Bethany ran down to
the basement kitchen to pass the news on
to Claire.

'We'd better phone home and say we'll
be late,' said Holly, remembering what her
mother had told her.

Bethany came up the stairs from the
kitchen, grinning like the Cheshire cat.

'Old Sourpuss!' she said to them with a
giggle. 'That's upset her for the rest of
the day.'

'May we use a phone?' asked Miranda. 'So
we can tell our parents where we are.' She
grinned at Holly and Peter. 'And I hope
Becky or Rachel pick up the phone so I can tell
them exactly where I am and what I'm doing!'
Becky and Rachel were Miranda's twin older
sisters, and they were a total pain!

'Of course,' said Bethany. 'You can use
the phone in Dad's study.' She led them
to the study door and opened it without
knocking.

They followed her in. Maurice was sitting

at his desk, staring at a letter which he had obviously just opened. His face was white and drawn. It looked like the letter contained some bad news.

'Dad?' said Bethany. 'Can they phone home?'

Maurice started and stared at her as if coming out of a nightmare.

'You'll have to leave,' he said sharply. 'I'm sorry. You'll all have to go home.' He threw the letter down and stood up. He came round the desk, his arms stretched in front of him as if he intended to push them out of the room.

Whatever news he had received in that letter, Holly realised, its effect on the actor had been devastating.

**Conclusive evidence**

Thirty seconds later, the Mystery Kids found themselves outside on the pavement. Maurice Harty hadn't exactly thrown them out, but he had certainly been very insistent that they should leave.

As they were being herded to the front door, Holly pulled out a pen and quickly managed to write her phone number on the back of Bethany's hand.

'Phone me,' she whispered. The anxious-looking young girl had nodded.

The three friends plodded gloomily along Benedict Avenue.

'What do you think was in that letter?' asked Miranda. 'It must have been something pretty horrible.'

'I know exactly what it was,' said Holly. 'And so do you, if you think about it.'

'I'll bet it was from that—' Peter began, but he was interrupted by Miranda.

'From that woman!' she yelped. 'From the woman in the park.'

'Probably demanding to know what happened to the money,' added Holly. 'And probably threatening him with all sorts of terrible things if he doesn't pay up.'

'So, what's our next move?' asked Peter.

'Home for tea, I guess,' said Miranda.

'I mean about Mr Harty,' said Peter.

'I left my phone number with Bethany,' said Holly. 'I think our best bet is to wait for her to contact us.'

'Are you sure?' asked Peter. 'I mean, she's only a kid.'

'Oh, yeah?' said Miranda. 'A kid who knows stuff you don't know! Fancy not knowing who Arthur Wrigglesworth was! Any fool knows that!'

'Arthur *Wellesley*!' said Peter.

'Same difference,' Miranda said airily. 'Anyway, all I'm saying is that she's a clever kid. Holly's right, we should wait for her to phone.'

'And let's hope she phones soon,' said Holly.

\* \* \*

77

Holly didn't have to wait long. She hadn't been home from school for more than half an hour the following afternoon when the phone rang.

'Holly?'

'Yes. Is that Bethany?'

'Yes.'

'How's your father?'

'I can't talk now. Creepy's prowling around. We need to meet. There's a snack bar near where I live. I'll give you the details.'

Bethany's voice was urgent and hissy, as though her mouth was close to the receiver for fear of being overheard. Holly took down the details of where the snack bar was.

'I'll be there in ten minutes,' she said.

No sooner had she put the receiver down than she was back on the phone to summon Miranda and Peter.

'Mum,' she called from the hall. 'I'm just going out to see Peter and Miranda, OK?'

'Don't be late,' called her mother. 'Behave yourselves and don't get into any trouble.'

Mrs Adams often asked Holly not to get into trouble. It never seemed to make much difference. Holly seemed to attract mysteries like a magnet.

The snack bar was a neat, clean little place just under a railway bridge. It had a few round tables and a high bar that ran alongside the front window. As Holly arrived, she saw Bethany sitting at the bar on a tall stool, sucking orange juice through a straw from a huge paper cup.

'Holly!' said Bethany in obvious relief. 'I gave Dad the money and—'

'Wait,' said Holly. 'Miranda and Peter are coming. You can tell us all at the same time.'

It wasn't long before Miranda arrived, and Peter was only a couple of minutes behind her.

'OK,' said Bethany as the four of them crammed themselves together along the bar. 'I gave Dad the envelope with the money in it. But he said it wasn't anything to do with him.'

'What?' said Miranda. 'But we saw him with it. Didn't he read our note about the woman coming to collect the envelope? Didn't you tell him?'

'Of course I did, but I didn't give him your note – just the money,' said Bethany. 'He told me he'd found the envelope on the underground train. He was going to take it to the police, but he realised he must have dropped it.'

'He didn't drop it,' said Holly. 'He hid it in a tree.'

'I didn't mention that you'd seen him do that,' said Bethany. 'Anyway, he took the envelope and said he'd take it to the police station.'

'You don't really believe that, do you?' asked Peter.

'Of course not,' said Bethany. She put her hand in her pocket. 'I want to show you something,' she said.

The thing she pulled out was a cheque-book stub.

'I got this out of my dad's desk,' she said. She looked solemnly at them. 'I don't want you thinking I'm some sort of sneak who goes prying through other people's things. You see, my dad always gets me to help him with financial things. He's a total dummy when it comes to anything to do with

80

numbers. So I do all the cross-checking when bank statements come. He calls me his little accountant.'

'Doesn't your mum do it?' asked Miranda. 'My mum does all the money stuff in our house.'

'When it comes to maths, my mum makes my dad look like Einstein,' said Bethany. 'I'm the only one in the family who can even add up. But the point is that Dad's been keeping his cheque-books away from me for the past few weeks. Hiding them from me, and when I'd say "Shall we sort the money out," he'd say "Not right now; we'll do it later." So last night I had a good search, and I found *this*.'

She put the cheque-book down on the bar. There were no cheques left in it. Bethany flicked through the narrow stubs.

'There!' she said, flattening the book back. 'See that?'

The three friends craned forwards. Scribbled on the stub was the word 'Cash' and the figure of two thousand pounds.

'And here,' said Bethany, flicking over a few stubs. Cash again, and another two thousand pounds. 'There are four of these big

81

cash withdrawals over the past few weeks. And the last one was two days ago.'

'The day we saw him with the envelope,' said Miranda. 'So it's not just a couple of thousand pounds. It's *eight* thousand pounds!'

'So far,' said Peter. 'And if he keeps on paying up, the blackmailers will just keep on demanding more.'

'Did you manage to find out what was in the letter he got yesterday?' asked Holly.

'Yes,' said Bethany. 'He tore it up but I managed to fit all the pieces back together again. It said: "You are only allowed one mistake. I want the money. Remember the drummer boy. Same time tomorrow or you know what will happen."'

'Same time tomorrow?' echoed Peter. 'That must mean the blackmailer wants your father to hand over more money tomorrow, at the same time, and in the same way, I suppose.'

'Not *tomorrow*!' said Miranda. 'It was tomorrow yesterday. I mean, today was tomorrow yesterday. So it's tomorrow *today*!'

'Let's think,' said Holly, looking at her

watch. 'Your dad goes through Belair Park in about half an hour from now, usually. That gives us plenty of time to get there and be waiting. And this time we'll follow the woman after she's taken the money.'

'I've been thinking,' said Bethany. 'What about this drummer boy? Do you think that can have anything to do with the blackmail? And I still want to know what my dad was up to in the garden that night.'

'Burying some evidence, maybe?' suggested Miranda. 'Perhaps we should go and investigate?'

'OK,' said Holly. 'Here's the plan. Peter goes to the park and waits for the money to be handed over. It's better if there's only one of us, anyway. That will mean there's less chance of us being seen.'

'Then I follow the woman and find out where she goes,' said Peter. 'And report back.'

'Exactly,' said Holly. 'And while Peter's doing that, the rest of us try and find out what Bethany's dad was doing in the garden.' She looked at Bethany. 'Is Claire going to be a problem?'

'Not if we're careful,' said Bethany. 'She thinks I'm over at a friend's house. If we can get through to the garden without her hearing, we shouldn't have any trouble with her.'

Holly stood up. 'OK, guys,' she said. 'Operation Save John Raven is underway. Let's get on with it!'

**Discovered**

Bethany led Holly and Miranda on tiptoe along the hallway.

'We'll go out through the French windows in Dad's study,' whispered Bethany. 'Creepy Crawly is probably down in the kitchen.'

Holly put her mouth close to Bethany's ear. 'I think I can hear voices.'

The three of them crept to the back of the house. Holly peered round the corner and down the stairway to the kitchen. Claire was there with another woman. There was something hushed and urgent about the way they were speaking to each other. As though they were exchanging deadly secrets.

The other woman was smartly dressed in a navy blue skirt and jacket with a white blouse. Holly thought she was probably in her early thirties, with a narrow, bony face and well-groomed shoulder-length dark brown hair.

'I'll go now,' said the other woman. 'Mustn't be late for my appointment. Hand me my coat, please.'

Holly ducked back and the three of them scampered soft-footed to the safety of Maurice Harty's study.

They heard the woman walk past and heard the front door close. Holly gave Bethany a description of the woman, but the young girl didn't seem to know who she was.

They made their way out into the long garden.

'OK,' said Miranda. 'Where did you see your dad digging?'

'Down here,' said Bethany, picking her way across a crazy-paved path between two great bushes of pampas grass.

Holly was very impressed by the garden. There was a central lawn surrounded by various flowerbeds, and a couple of tall poplar trees at the far end, which attractively framed the spire of the church.

It made her own small square garden at home seem very inadequate. One of the dreams of which her parents often spoke was of moving out of London and finding themselves a home with a huge, long garden.

Bethany disappeared into a small shed and came back out with a spade. She led them down under the cool shade of the trees.

'He was here,' she said. It was obvious that the soil had been disturbed recently. Bethany held out the spade for Holly.

'Miranda likes digging,' said Holly.

'I do?' said Miranda, taking the spade.

'Of course you do,' said Holly. 'Besides which, you're stronger than I am.'

'If you say so,' Miranda said good-naturedly as she dug the blade of the spade into the soft earth and gave it a good stamp with her foot.

She had only shifted six or seven spade-loads of soil before she struck something hard. At first she thought it was a stone, but as she scraped the blade of the spade across it, they could all see that it was something smooth and flat.

Holly crouched down, scooping up earth from around the object with her hands. The thing she pulled out of the shallow hole was an old biscuit tin with a picture of Santa Claus on it.

'That was from Gran, last Christmas,' said Bethany.

'It's only been in here a little while,' said Holly, brushing the dirt off the lid. 'This must have been what you saw your dad burying.'

'Open it,' Miranda said impatiently. 'I bet it's the answer to the entire thing!'

Holly took the lid off. Inside the tin was a bundle of rags. And inside the rags, as she lifted them out, was the beautiful gold-coloured model of the drummer boy.

'So he didn't sell it,' breathed Bethany. 'But why did he hide it?'

Holly held the exquisite model up to the sunlight. Every detail was perfect, from the cross-bands on the snare drum to the buttons on the boy's tunic. Even the little face was totally realistic, the eyes staring resolutely forwards and the jaw set with determination.

The three of them crouched round the hole, gazing at the golden drummer boy in astonished silence. Miranda glanced down at a movement by her foot. A long, fat worm was making its way across her shoe. She picked it up and felt its tickly wriggles in her hand.

'What should we do?' asked Bethany.

'Bethany! What are you doing down there!' came a shrill voice from the direction of the house. 'I've told you before about getting filthy and then treading it through the house!' It was Claire.

'I hate that woman!' breathed Bethany. 'She's always watching me! Don't let her see the model. I don't want her knowing anything about this.'

The three of them stood up. Bethany took the model from Holly and hid it behind her back. Claire Crawley came tottering down the lawn in her high-heeled shoes. She was in a short green dress, so tight that it looked as if someone had crammed her into it with half a litre of fat and a shoe-horn.

'What do you want?' asked Bethany. 'We're not doing anything.'

'I thought you were at Katie's house,' said Claire.

'I was,' said Bethany. 'I came back. OK?'

Claire stared at the hole and at the open tin with its filling of rags.

'What's that?' she asked.

'A tin,' said Bethany. 'What does it look like?'

Claire glared at her. 'Don't be so cheeky,' she said. 'What's it doing there?'

Bethany looked down at it. 'I don't see it doing anything,' she said. Miranda stifled a burst of laughter.

'What was in it?' asked Claire.

'Nothing,' said Bethany.

'Don't lie,' said Claire. 'What have you got hidden behind your back? Show me your hands!'

The three of them were standing facing her in a row, Bethany on the left, Holly in the middle and Miranda on the right. Bethany held out her empty left hand, and deftly handed the model to Holly with her right.

'The other hand!' demanded Claire.

Bethany displayed another empty hand to the irritated young woman.

Claire glared at Holly.

'You've got it!' she said.

'Me?' said Holly. 'I don't think I have.' She held up both grubby hands. 'See?'

'You!' said Claire, frowning at Miranda.

'I'm sick of these silly games. Give it to me at once!'

'Are you sure you want me to give it to you?' asked Miranda.

Claire held her hand out. 'I want it now!' she said.

'You won't like it,' said Miranda.

Claire made an impatient, demanding movement with her hand. Miranda brought her closed fist round. She held her hand above Claire's open palm and spread her fingers.

The worm landed in Claire's hand.

Claire let out a shriek as the worm slithered in her palm.

The three youngsters laughed as Claire shook the worm off with a grimace of distaste.

'Very funny,' Claire snarled. She gave each of them a devastating glare before turning and tottering back up the lawn.

'Nice one, Miranda,' said Bethany. 'That should teach Creepy Crawly to throw her weight about!'

'You know something,' said Miranda as she watched Claire make her unsteady way back to the house. 'In that green dress she looks like a sausage that's gone mouldy.'

She brought the model out from behind her back.

'Well, now,' she said. 'What are we going to do with this little fellow?'

'We need to find out more about it,' said Holly. She looked at Bethany. 'Your dad must have had a reason for hiding it. And we've got to find out what that reason was.'

'If we want to find out about it, I know who to ask,' said Bethany. 'Humpty-Dumpty!'

'Who?' Holly asked in surprise.

'Mr Humphrey,' said Bethany. 'He runs the model shop where my dad gets a lot of his soldiers. I'll bet he'll know about it. His shop's not all that far away. You could walk there in fifteen minutes.'

'That's not a bad idea,' said Holly. 'Tell you what, give me the directions, and I'll go over there right now. You and Miranda stay here with the model and wait for Peter. I'll be as quick as I can.'

'Don't tell Humpty-Dumpty that my dad's got the model,' said Bethany. 'Just give him a description of it and ask if there's anything special about it.'

Holly smiled at her. 'Good thinking,' she said. 'You'd make a first-rate detective.'

'I don't know about that,' said Bethany. 'I just want my dad to be back the way he was before all this started.'

'I know,' said Holly, giving her a quick hug. 'Now then, tell me how to get to Humpty-Dumpty's shop and I'll be off.'

Peter had tried various lurking-places while he waited for Maurice Harty. He'd hung about in corners in the underground station until the suspicious frowns of the woman in the ticket office had made him slink off.

Then he'd found a little nook just outside the station. It seemed the perfect place until the first train-load of disembarked passengers came herding out of the station. He couldn't see a thing as they swept past him. Maurice Harty could have done cartwheels across the park, and Peter wouldn't have known about it. The commuters hurried by, totally blocking his view.

He ended up hiding in the trees by the

south end of the path that Maurice had previously taken. He knew it would look a bit curious if anyone happened to glance in his direction and spot him peering through the low, hanging branches. But as they all seemed in such a hurry to get home, he didn't think much notice would be taken of him.

Time passed and Peter was just beginning to wonder whether Maurice would ever appear, when a familiar grey-coated figure broke away from the crowds leaving the underground station and headed for the park.

'Aha!' murmured Peter, sliding into deeper cover. 'Here he comes!'

Maurice Harty strode in his usual purposeful way along the path and into the trees. Peter detached himself from the tree he'd been leaning against and shadowed Maurice, keeping behind him and well out of sight.

Maurice came to a stop at the drinking fountain. Peter kept perfectly still, holding his breath as he saw Maurice stare slowly all around. There was no one else on the path. With a movement that startled Peter in its suddenness, Maurice darted into the trees.

Letting out a hiss of breath, Peter followed him. This was *it*! There was no doubt about it. Maurice was trotting through the trees, bypassing the thick bushes, and heading for that same tree where they had seen him put the envelope earlier that week.

*It's all up to me*, thought Peter.

The transfer of the thick envelope from Maurice's coat to the cleft in the tree was all over in a moment. If anything, Maurice was even more nervy than he had been the previous time. He stared around, as though double-checking that he wasn't being watched.

Peter hoped desperately that he wouldn't be seen. He held his breath. At one point Maurice Harty seemed to look straight through him before taking to his heels and vanishing into the trees.

'Whoo!' Peter let out a gasp. He slid down the tree trunk and settled himself on the ground in such a way that he could see Maurice's tree through a leafy spray of twigs that sprouted up from the ground.

A minute passed. Peter could hear the distant sounds of traffic and, closer by, the chatter of birds and occasional buzz of an insect. But there was no sign of the yellow-coated woman.

Peter frowned at his watch. He was sure she'd arrived more quickly than this last time. Had she seen him and been scared off? Peter was already composing Miranda's sarcastic comments in his head as he heard the faint rustle of movement.

It was the same woman. She was wearing the yellow coat and the headscarf. She moved across to the tree and reached up. This time her hand came down with something in it. And even at that distance, Peter could make out the padded shape of a brown envelope. A split second later she had tucked it away into her shoulder-bag.

She turned and walked rapidly back the way she had come. Peter gave her a few seconds before prising himself up and trotting slowly after her.

She came out of the south end of the trees. She walked very quickly across the grass, heading for the south-west exit from the park. Peter followed at a discreet distance.

*If Miranda were here*, he thought, *she'd*

*want to be dressed up like a bush or some-thing*!

But Peter realised he didn't need a disguise. Why should the woman suspect an ordinary schoolboy of knowing all about her criminal scheme?

She left the park and crossed the road. Once out of the park she slowed down a little.

*So*, thought Peter, *she thinks she's in the clear, does she? We'll see about that!*

The woman turned off the main road and Peter trailed her through a confusing network of back streets. Twice she crossed a road, making Peter duck into cover as she glanced round to check there was no traffic.

She came to a road with a long brick wall running the whole length of one side. Peter kept in cover until she turned the corner, then ran as fast as he could to catch up with her. She turned another corner and lost herself in the maze of residential roads.

He edged his head round the brickwork and nearly leaped clean out of his shoes as he found himself face to face with the woman. She'd taken her scarf off. She had shoulder length, dark brown hair and a sharp, bony face. There was anger in her eyes as she caught Peter by the collar and dragged him out into the open.

'OK,' she spat. 'What's the game? Why are you following me?'

Peter gulped as she twisted his collar. He hadn't been nearly so clever as he'd thought. And now he was well and truly caught!

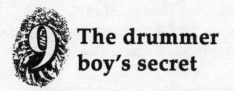

# The drummer boy's secret

Following Bethany's directions, Holly found herself approaching a small row of rather smart shops, set back from the road behind a wide pavement. There was an antiques dealer, a Thai restaurant, a fashion boutique, a jewellers, and there, at the far end, as Bethany had told her, was the shop she was looking for: Millenium Models.

The name was picked out in shiny chrome on a black background. Holly had expected something like a glorified toyshop and she was quite surprised at how impressive Millenium Models looked.

Holly stared in at the large window display. The window was divided into sections by glass shelves. Some shelves held boxes: model aeroplane kits, battleships and cars. Then there were trains and fire engines and coaches. And marching endlessly along the two top shelves were entire battalions of soldiers, just like the ones Holly had seen on display in Maurice Harty's study.

A bell tinkled as Holly entered the shop. It was brightly lit and filled with more shelves.

*Jamie would love this place*, Holly thought as she gazed at model race tracks and train sets and remote-controlled aeroplanes.

A small bald-headed man stood behind the counter, his head just showing above glass display cases filled with yet more soldiers.

'Hello,' Holly said brightly as she walked up to the counter. 'I wonder if you can help me.'

'I can try,' said the man.

'This shop was recommended to me,' said Holly. 'Are you Humpt – er, Mr Humphrey?'

'That's right.' The man had a friendly smile. He reminded Holly of a cheerful cartoon mole. 'Like the joke about the camel.'

'Sorry?'

The shopkeeper beamed at her. 'What do you call a camel with three humps? Humphrey!' The little man grinned at her.

Holly laughed politely. That joke was so old it ought to have a long white beard!

'I'm looking for a model soldier,' said Holly.

'Ye-es?' said Mr Humphrey, his eyes rolling around the shop. 'Any particular type? An Arthurian knight, perhaps? Or an American Civil War Rebel? I've got a lovely one of General Lee on Traveller.'

'Not really,' said Holly. 'I'm looking for something Napoleonic. A drummer boy.'

'Hmm.' Mr Humphrey came round the counter. He was as round as a rubber ball. He doubled over and peered into a display case.

'I was told there was a special model,' Holly said cautiously. 'I think they said it was painted gold.'

Mr Humphrey straightened up and gave her a curious look. '*Painted* gold? Are you talking about the Farocher drummer boy?'

Holly smiled hopefully. 'I don't know. Am I?'

'What do you know about the model?' asked Mr Humphrey.

'Not much,' said Holly. She held her hands

apart, one above the other. 'It's about this high.' She gave a brief description of the model.

Mr Humphrey's eyes narrowed. 'Have you seen one of these?' he asked.

'A friend of mine has,' said Holly. 'Why? Would it be valuable?'

'If it's a solid gold Gustav Farocher drummer boy, it's worth a lot of money,' said Mr Humphrey. 'I should know. I had one on display in my window up until a month ago.'

'Oh! What happened?'

'It was stolen,' said Mr Humphrey. 'Someone broke in here in the middle of the night and stole it.'

'Oh, crumbs!' gasped Holly. 'How awful! And did you say *solid* gold?'

'That's right,' said Mr Humphrey. 'Although I wouldn't get excited if I were you. The one your friend saw was probably only a replica. There are a lot of them about.'

'How would a person be able to tell?' asked Holly.

'The initials "GF" would be on the base of a real one,' said Mr Humphrey. 'But don't get your hopes up. An original Farocher drummer boy is worth several thousand pounds. Hey, wait a moment! Where are you going?'

But Holly didn't have time to explain, even if she could have explained. She needed to get back to Maurice Harty's house and find out if that golden drummer boy they had dug up out of the garden was what she thought it was.

Miranda and Bethany were up in the young girl's bedroom. Bethany was sitting cross-legged on her bed with the golden model soldier in her lap.

Miranda was pacing up and down, picking her way through the debris on Bethany's floor as she marched from wall to wall.

She looked at her watch for the twentieth time. Patience wasn't one of Miranda's more obvious virtues.

'Shouldn't your dad be home by now?'

Bethany looked unhappily at her bedside clock. 'He's usually home before this,' she said. She looked at Miranda. 'What are we going to do?'

'I'm not sure,' said Miranda. She smiled reassuringly. 'Holly will think of something, don't worry.'

'Why did Dad bury this in the garden?' She looked down at the drummer boy.

'Because he didn't want anyone to know he had it?' suggested Miranda.

'That's exactly what I was thinking,' said Bethany. 'You know I said Dad has been having these blackouts?'

'Yes, I remember,' said Miranda.

'Well, the day after I found him on the floor in his study with his outdoor clothes on, was the day I saw him with *this*.' She held up the drummer boy. She looked uneasily at Miranda. 'Suppose these blackouts that Dad is having are like . . . like sleepwalking? What if he does things and then can't remember them?'

'That doesn't sound very likely,' said Miranda.

'No?' said Bethany. 'So how come Dad couldn't remember putting his coat on that night? He said the last thing he remembered was getting into bed. But I found him *fully clothed* and with his coat on.'

'OK, I see what you mean,' said Miranda. 'But what are you getting at?'

'If Dad could dress himself and come downstairs without remembering anything about it, why couldn't he go out of the house and do things?'

'What sort of things are you thinking of?' asked Miranda.

Bethany held the drummer boy out to her. 'Break into someone's house and steal something valuable?' she said. 'What if this isn't just gold paint? What if it's solid gold?'

'I can't believe your dad's a thief,' said Miranda. 'No way!'

'So why did he bury it in the garden?' asked Bethany. 'Don't you see? It makes sense. *That* could be why he's being black-mailed! Someone knows he stole this model.' Bethany shook her head. 'I don't mean Dad's a thief. I don't think that at all. But maybe he's doing bad things without knowing anything about it.'

'It's possible, I suppose,' Miranda said thoughtfully. 'But if that's the case, we've got to do something about it.'

'I know,' said Bethany. 'I'm going to! I've

decided! I'm going to phone Dr Bartholemew. He's our family doctor. I'm going to tell him the whole story. He'll know what to do!'

There was a soft, sharp click from over by the door.

'What was that?' asked Miranda.

The click was followed by the rattle of heels running down the stairs. Bethany threw the soldier down and dived for the door. She swung on the handle.

'Creepy Crawly!' she screamed. 'She must have been listening! She's locked us in!'

Miranda leaped to the door and joined Bethany in trying to get it open. The handle turned easily enough, but the door was locked tight.

'Oi!' shouted Miranda, hammering on the door. 'Let us out of here!'

'Why should she lock us in?' said Bethany. 'Unless . . . oh! Her hand came up over her mouth. 'It was her! It was her all the time! *She's* been blackmailing Dad!'

Peter's mind was racing. The woman's grip was vice-like on his collar and there didn't seem much hope of him being able to squirm free.

She brought her face closer to his.

'Why are you following me?' Her voice was snake-like; cold and cruel.

'I was too shy,' wailed Peter. He adopted what his father called his 'little boy lost' expression.

'What?' spat the woman. 'What are you talking about?'

'I wanted to ask you for your autograph,' Peter blurted, hoping he was making himself sound quite innocent and maybe a little silly. 'You *are* Mary Miller, aren't you? From *One Step Ahead*?'

The idea had come into his head like an arrow out of nowhere. The woman did look a little like the actor who played the role of the mother in the television show. Peter knew perfectly well that it wasn't her, but he hoped she might think he was daft enough to believe she was.

'I'm not Mary Miller,' said the woman. Peter noticed that her voice was instantly less aggressive.

Peter stared wide-eyed at her. 'Honest?' he

said. 'You look just like her. My dad says Mary Miller is the most gorgeous woman on TV. You're really not her?'

The woman's grip relaxed on his collar and a half-smile played at the corner of her mouth.

'No, I'm not her,' she said, smoothing Peter's clothes out with her hand. 'And you really shouldn't follow women around, you know, even if you do think they look like television stars.'

It had worked! She'd completely fallen for it!

Peter gave her a silly smile. 'I'm really sorry,' he said. 'I feel so stupid!'

'No harm done,' said the woman. 'You'd better get off home.'

Peter nodded and, without another word, ran back round the corner.

He glanced round to check she wasn't watching, but the coast was clear.

'*Yesss!*' He gave a leap, punching the air with his fist. If only Holly and Miranda – *especially* Miranda – had been there to see it! Pure, brilliant brain-work!

He came to a panting halt and turned,

running back to the corner and cautiously edging an eye round the wall. The woman in the yellow coat was walking rapidly away.

Suddenly she turned and stepped through some tall black iron railings that fronted one of the houses. As Peter watched, he saw her disappear downwards, walking down steps into a basement flat.

He gave it a few seconds then trotted along the street. They were tall houses, with long stone steps up to the front doors. And most of the houses had second entrances down steps to a basement.

The woman had gone into number 23B. Peter made a mental note. Talk about first-rate detective work! Without any help from the two girls, he'd cracked the entire case!

He was just plotting in his head the quickest route back to Benedict Avenue when a red hatchback car drove into sight. Peter almost choked in shock. He'd know that car any-where. And he'd know the driver, too. A woman with a tumbling mass of golden hair and a huge, bright red mouth.

It was Claire Crawley!

There was no time to think. Peter acted

instinctively to get out of sight. At the top of the stone steps was a small walled area with a large wheelybin standing in it. He took a quick glance to check no one was watching, then lifted the wheelybin's lid. It was empty. He climbed up on to the low brick wall and hopped down into the black interior of the rubbish bin.

The lid came banging down. He crouched uncomfortably in the bin, his ears pricking for any sound. He heard the car draw up nearby and a second or two later there was the noise of the door being closed.

The inside of the bin smelt horrible. Peter tried not to breathe too much, preferring not to think exactly what it was that he was smelling.

He heard the sharp *click*, *click*, *click*, of Claire Crawley's heels. They were coming towards him. His first thought had been right. She *was* coming here.

The clicking heels came to a halt right beside the bin.

Peter held his breath. He heard the sound of a door being opened below him.

'What are you doing here?' He recognised

the voice. It was the woman in the yellow coat.

'We've got to talk, Tessa,' said Claire. 'There's trouble with the kid. I think she's figured it out.'

'Shut up, you fool!' spat the woman called Tessa. Peter could hear from her voice that she was coming up the steps. 'Do you want the whole world to know?'

'I'm sorry,' said Claire. 'But I'm worried we're going to get caught!'

'OK,' said Tessa. 'Come down and we'll talk about it. Just give me one second to deal with *this*!'

And then the worst thing imaginable happened. The lid was lifted up off the wheelybin. Peter's hiding place had been discovered.

**Where is Maurice Harty?**

Holly ran as fast as she could, her shoes pounding on the pavement as she sped towards Benedict Avenue.

She hated the thoughts that were spinning in her brain. But she couldn't stop herself thinking. Even though those thoughts made her heart sink right down to her toes.

There was only one explanation. Maurice Harty had stolen the drummer boy. Someone had found out about the theft and was blackmailing him. That was the only explanation that seemed to Holly to make any sense.

But she had to know for certain. Until she had actually seen the letters 'G F' on the base of the golden model, there was still a shred of hope that she was wrong.

She came hurtling round the corner into

Benedict Avenue, ignoring the stitch that was eating into her side. She ran across the road.

She saw the car out of the corner of her eye. Normally Holly was very careful about road safety, but this time she had stupidly run out into the road without looking.

She had a split second to throw herself forwards as the car drove towards her. She felt air rush by as the car passed only centimetres away from her.

She stared after it, expecting the driver to bring it to a screeching halt, expecting to be shouted at for her lack of care. But the red hatchback didn't stop. It speeded up and went round the curve with a wail of protesting tyres.

'Claire!' breathed Holly, her heart pounding in her chest. She had only caught a glimpse of the mass of golden hair, but there was no mistaking the car.

Gathering her wits, Holly turned and ran towards Maurice Harty's house. What on earth could have happened there for Claire to be speeding away like that?

Holly rang the bell furiously. There was no

answer. She rang again then crouched and called through the letter-box.

'Bethany! Miranda! Hello! Is there anyone there?'

Nothing!

Holly ran round to the side of the house. She climbed on to the low dividing wall and jumped up at the door which led to the side alley. She hooked a leg over the top of the door and eased herself over and down into the alley. A few seconds later she was running down to the back of the house.

The French windows were shut tight. Holly stumbled across to the back door. She gave a gasp of relief as the door opened. She ran into the house, shouting for Miranda or Bethany.

The house seemed horribly silent. She came to the foot of the stairs and shouted again.

'Miranda!'

'Hoi!' Holly heard the faint response coming from the top of the house. With a shout of relief she pounded up the stairs. Now she could hear Miranda and Bethany, yelling and hammering on the locked door.

'It's OK!' called Holly as she tore up the last flight of stairs. 'I'm here!'

The key was still in the lock. She turned it and the door flew open.

All three of them started talking at once.

'Wait!' howled Holly. 'One at a time!'

Miranda took a deep breath. 'Claire locked us in. She heard Bethany say she was going to call their doctor and tell him everything.'

'I think Dad stole the drummer boy,' said Bethany. 'During one of his blackouts.'

'And Claire must be involved in the blackmailing!' added Miranda. 'Otherwise why would she lock us in?'

'Where's the model?' Holly asked urgently. 'I need to see it!'

'Never mind that; where's Claire?' demanded Miranda. 'We've got to get her!'

'Too late,' said Holly. 'She's gone. She nearly ran me over. Show me the model.'

Bethany ran to her bed and scooped up the drummer boy.

Holly took it from her and turned it over. Engraved on the base were the letters 'G F'.

'What does that mean?' asked Miranda.

'I'll explain in a minute,' said Holly. 'But

115

I think Bethany's idea was right. We should phone for help. Like, *now*!'

Bethany nodded and ran down the stairs.

Miranda grabbed Holly's arm. 'There's something else,' she said. 'I didn't want to mention it in front of Bethany, but her father should have been home ages ago.'

'Maybe he's been delayed,' said Holly.

'Of course he has,' said Miranda. 'But by what?'

Holly had no answer to that question.

They followed Bethany down the stairs. A door stood open and they could see Bethany in the room beyond. It was a bedroom. Holly assumed it must belong to Maurice Harty and his wife.

Bethany was standing by the double bed with a phone receiver to her ear.

She looked around. 'It's dead,' she said blankly, holding the receiver out towards them.

'I'm sure it isn't,' said Miranda. She took it and jabbed her finger up and down on the cut-off button. 'Oh!' She looked at Holly. 'It is!'

'Claire must have cut the phone line before

she ran out,' said Holly. 'Now, listen! I've got to tell you what I found out at the model shop.'

She quickly explained about the model, showing them the engraved letters on the base to confirm her words.

'That proves Dad stole it!' cried Bethany. 'But he couldn't have known what he was doing!' Her voice broke with emotion. 'What are we going to do?'

'Which one is Claire's room?' asked Holly. She put her hands on Bethany's shaking shoulders. 'Come on, Bethany, be brave.'

Bethany slowly wiped her eyes with her sleeve. 'I *am* being brave,' she said. 'I'm being very brave, if you ask me.' She gave a sniff. 'What did you want to know?'

'Claire's room?' said Holly.

Bethany nodded. She led them back up one flight of stairs and into a small bedroom with pine furnishings and a single bed.

'OK,' said Holly. 'Look around. See if you can find anything.'

'Like what?' asked Miranda as she gazed around the oddly spotless room.

'Like something to link Claire with the

woman in the yellow coat,' said Holly. 'An address book or letters or something like that.'

Bethany went over to the wardrobe and pulled the door open. Empty hangers rattled together.

'Her clothes are gone,' said Bethany.

Miranda ran to the chest of drawers and opened a drawer. 'Empty!' she said.

'And there was make-up stuff, too,' said Bethany. 'She's taken everything.'

'She's done a runner!' said Miranda.

'In Dad's car!' exclaimed Bethany.

Holly spotted something down by the side of the bed. She stooped and picked it up. It was a brown phial with a white label on it. The sort of container that a pharmacist keeps pills in. Holly took the plastic lid off. There were a few yellow and white capsules inside.

'I wonder what these are,' she said, tipping them out into her hand. The other two came over to look at them.

'I'm not certain,' said Miranda. 'I mean, don't take my word on this, but I know what they *look* like. They look just like some pills my aunt was taking a while back when she was under a lot of stress.'

Holly looked at her. 'What were they for?'

'They were sleeping-pills,' said Miranda. 'Very powerful sleeping-pills.'

Peter cowered in the bottom of the wheelybin, convinced that at any moment a hand would come down and pluck him out like a winkle out of its shell.

But it wasn't a hand that came down. The light was blotted out and something large and heavy and lumpy was dropped on his head.

'OK,' said the woman in the yellow coat, the woman Claire had called Tessa. 'That's got rid of that. Come down and tell me what's happened.'

'We should get out of here,' said Claire. 'This place is too close to Benedict Avenue. I've got all my stuff in the car. We should get right out of London, before they find us.'

'Stop panicking,' came Tessa's receding voice. 'I mean to get a lot more money out of Harty before I finish with him. So, come on, tell me exactly what's happened.'

There was the sound of a door closing and then nothing.

Peter lifted his arms up. He didn't need to be a genius to figure out what had happened. Tessa had dumped a bag of rubbish on top of him. He felt over the lumps and bumps that pressed down on him.

'Yuck!' His fingers met something sticky. He pulled away and a cascade of horrible stuff came pouring out of a rip in the bottom of the bag. He held his breath as all sorts of household rubbish fell into his lap.

He waited until the stuff stopped falling and then squirmed, pushing upwards past the half-empty bag, his mouth shut tight as he did his best not to breathe.

He lifted the lid a couple of centimetres and peered out. There didn't seem to be anyone about. With a shudder he clambered up over the broken rubbish bag. He shook pieces of potato peel and soggy tea-bags off his clothes.

He looked round. A woman with a child in a pushchair was coming up the road. She stared at him in amazement.

'Household waste inspection,' said Peter,

jumping out of the bin and peeling a sticky piece of something-or-other off his jeans. 'That one's fine. Nice class of rubbish. Ten out of ten.' He was backing away all the while.

The woman opened her mouth to say something, but Peter took to his heels before she got the chance.

As he ran, he tried not to worry about what he must smell like. There were things that had to be done before he could go home for a shower and a change of clothes. And the first thing was to get back to Benedict Avenue and let Maurice Harty know the address of his blackmailer. And the fact that Claire Crawley was involved!

He was breathless by the time he ran up the front path of Maurice Harty's house. He threw himself on the doorbell. It rang loudly through the house as he leaned his thumb on it.

The door opened after a few seconds.

'Peter!' gasped Holly. 'At last!' She stared at him. 'You've got orange peel in your hair.'

'Never mind that,' Peter gasped, pushing over the threshold. 'I've got to speak to

Maurice Harty! The plan worked! I know where she lives!'

Miranda was just behind Holly in the hall.

'Claire is involved!' she shouted.

'What?' yelled Peter. 'I was just going to tell *you* that! How did you find out?'

'It's a long story,' said Holly. 'Claire's gone.'

'And I know where,' said Peter. 'She's with the other woman right now. The woman in the yellow coat. I've got to tell Maurice!'

'He isn't here,' said Holly. 'We haven't seen him.'

Peter stared at her. 'He must be,' he said. 'He left the envelope in the tree ages ago.'

Bethany was standing on the stairs. 'Something must have happened to him!' she said. 'He'd be home by now, otherwise. Something *bad* must have happened to him!'

Holly looked anxiously at her friends. She didn't want to admit it in front of the frightened girl, but it did look as if Bethany was right. There was really only one explanation for why Maurice Harty hadn't arrived home yet.

Between Belair Park and Benedict Avenue, something had happened to him. And, under the circumstances, Holly was afraid that it must have been something bad.

## 11  The battle of Benedict Avenue

Peter closed the front door and the four of them stood staring at one another in the hallway.

'We've got to think!' said Holly. 'We've got to think of the best thing to do.'

'Call Dr Bartholomew,' said Bethany.

'Call the police!' said Miranda. Her nose twitched. 'What's that funny smell?'

'It's me,' said Peter. 'Just don't ask!'

'I think Miranda's right about the police,' said Holly. 'Something must have happened to Maurice. They must have done something to him.'

'They?' said Peter. 'Who's *they*?'

'They the blackmailers,' exclaimed Miranda. 'What other they is there? Why do you smell like a compost heap, Peter?'

'I told you not to ask! Look, I saw the whole

thing,' said Peter. 'Mr Harty left the money. The woman picked it up and went to a flat in Mandrake Street. That's where I've just come from. There's no way she can have done anything to Mr Harty. And Claire is with her right now! Claire thinks Bethany has sussed something out. She's running! We've got to find Mr Harty.' He looked at Bethany. 'Has your dad got any friends nearby? Any neighbours he might be visiting?'

'A few,' said Bethany. 'We need his address book.'

She ran into the study, and the rest of them followed. She threw herself into the chair and opened the drawer in the middle of the desk. She pulled out a large black leather book.

'Phone numbers,' she said. 'We can phone – *oh, heck*! We can't! The phone isn't working.'

'It isn't?' said Peter. 'How come?'

'Creepy pulled out the wires,' said Miranda. 'She locked us in Bethany's room and then yanked the phone wires out to make double sure she'd have time to escape.'

'She didn't reckon on me turning up so soon,' said Holly. She frowned. 'Bethany?, can you think of any particular place where your father might go? Somewhere nearby? A pub, maybe?'

Bethany shook her head.

'There might be something in his private box,' she said. She looked round at them. 'He keeps all his most private papers in a special box. I'm on my word of honour not ever to open it.'

'Where is it?' asked Miranda.

Bethany leaned over and pulled open the bottom right hand drawer. Inside was a dark blue metal box.

'I promised never to open it, though,' said Bethany.

'There might be something important inside,' said Peter. 'I'm sure you'd be allowed to break your promise if it helped your dad.'

Bethany thought for a moment then shook her head. 'I promised,' she said simply.

'But you never promised not to let someone else open it, did you?' said Miranda. 'Peter, don't stand so close. You smell horrible!'

'No-o, I didn't promise that,' said Bethany.

Her face brightened and she lifted the box out of the drawer and handed it to Holly.

Holly laid it on the desk and turned the key. The box was filled with all sorts of official-looking papers and documents, but on the very top was a folded sheet of writing paper.

Holly opened it. It was typewritten. She read it aloud.

'"Dear Mr Harty. You are a thief! You were seen stealing that toy soldier from Millenium Models. Unless you pay me ten thousand pounds, I will go to the police and your acting career will be over. Don't think for one moment that I won't do it. I will make it easy for you, so I don't want to hear about you having any trouble getting the money. You will leave the money in amounts of two thousand pounds each week for the next five weeks in an oak tree in Belair Park. Take your usual path home, but leave the path and go into the trees to the left. You will see the tree I mean. It is an oak that stands alone and which has a cleft trunk. Put an envelope in the cleft and go away immediately. If you fail to comply with this demand, I shall have no hesitation in letting the police know all about you."'

'So it *is* true,' Peter said flatly. He looked from face to unhappy face. 'Miranda's right,' he said. 'We should call the police.'

'But Dad didn't know what he was doing!' said Bethany. 'He wouldn't steal anything. It's because of these blackouts.'

'How long has he been having the blackouts, Bethany?' asked Miranda.

'Not long,' said Bethany. 'A few weeks, I think.'

'And how long has Claire been looking after you?' asked Miranda. Holly looked curiously at her. Miranda seemed to be following some particular train of thought.

'Since Mum went off to America,' said Bethany.

'And that was a few weeks ago as well, right?' said Miranda.

'Yes, of course, but—' Bethany's voice stopped dead as Miranda pulled the brown phial of capsules out of her pocket.

'I think these are very strong sleeping-tablets,' she said. 'We just found them in Claire's bedroom. If these are anything like the ones my aunt took, they're strong enough to knock a person out cold for eight hours or more.'

'What are you getting at?' asked Peter.

'Don't you think it's a bit of a coincidence that Maurice should start having blackouts at the same time as Claire arrives?' Miranda asked. 'And don't you think it's even more of a coincidence that she should have a bottle of heavy-duty sleeping-tablets?'

'You mean you think she's been dosing Maurice up with sleeping-pills?' said Holly. 'But if he's been zonked out on pills, how can he have robbed that shop?'

'Exactly!' said Miranda. 'He can't!'

'But he had the drummer boy,' said Bethany. 'How did it get here?'

'Look,' said Miranda. 'The way I see it, the whole thing was carefully planned by Claire and this other woman.'

'Her name's Tessa,' said Peter. 'I heard Claire call her Tessa.'

'Tessa!' Bethany almost shrieked. 'The woman who recommended Claire was called Tessa. Tessa Burke. She works at the same studio as Dad.'

'That's it!' said Holly. 'That's the final link. Tessa gets Claire the job here so she can dish out sleeping-pills to Maurice without him knowing about it.'

'In his late night cocoa!' said Bethany. 'She always made him a mug of cocoa last thing at night.'

'And while he's fast asleep one night, Tessa robs the model shop,' said Miranda. 'Then Claire lets her into the house. They dress Maurice and put his coat on. Then they stick the stolen model in his pocket and leave him in a heap on the carpet.'

'He wakes up with no idea what's going on,' said Holly. 'He finds the drummer boy, and before he has a chance to work out what's going on, he gets a letter from the blackmailers.'

'And he really believes he did it!' said Peter. 'So he pays up to keep them quiet!'

Holly looked solemnly at her friends. 'He should have gone to the police. I wish he had! I'm sure they'd have realised it wasn't his fault, even if they couldn't have known that the blackouts were being caused by Claire.'

'But then everyone would have thought he

was ill,' said Bethany. 'He could have lost his job!'

'Now we really have got to call the police!' said Peter.

'Shouldn't we try to find Maurice first?' asked Miranda. 'Then he can tell the police.'

'That takes us right back to square one,' said Holly. 'Where on earth do we start looking?'

'What's that stain down your sleeve?' Miranda asked Peter. 'How the heck did you get in such a mess?'

'I hid in a wheelybin and I got rubbish chucked all over me, OK?' snapped Peter. 'Satisfied now?'

'It figures,' grinned Miranda. 'That could only happen to you.'

'Can we get back to the business in hand?' asked Peter. 'How are we going to find Mr Harty?'

Before anyone had the chance to respond to Peter's question, a sound from the hallway made them all freeze. It was the distinctive sound of a key in the front door.

'Dad!' gasped Bethany, jumping up and running to the study door.

Holly caught hold of her arm. 'Wait!' she whispered. 'It might not be. Listen!'

They stood in complete silence as they heard the front door swing open and then close.

Then they all heard a sound they recognised only too well. The sharp, staccato *click, click, click* of high heels on the polished floorboards of the hallway.

'Hello? Mr Harty?' It was Claire's voice. 'Hello? Are you home?'

Holly and her friends kept absolutely silent behind the study door.

'He's not here,' they heard Claire say in a quieter voice.

'Good,' said another voice. A voice which Peter recognised at once. Tessa's voice. 'Now get up there and find those tablets, you stupid fool!'

'Don't call me names,' said Claire. 'Where would you be without me? Who's been doing all the dirty work around here?'

'Oh, shut up!' snarled Tessa. 'While we're here you'd better go and check on the two kids you locked up. Make sure they haven't got out.'

'They won't have got out,' said Claire. 'Not unless they opened a window and jumped!' They heard her go clattering up the stairs.

But a couple of seconds later something happened which sent four hearts leaping up into four throats. As they stared at each other in dismay, they heard footsteps approaching the study door.

Tessa was heading straight for the room in which they were hiding.

**All wrapped up**

Holly only had a few moments to act. A plan had formed in her mind, but if it was going to work, it would mean perfect timing from all four of them. Not to mention a good deal of luck.

She grabbed the bottle of pills from Miranda and thrust them into Bethany's hand.

'Lie over there,' she whispered, pointing at the floor beyond the Persian carpet. 'Pretend to be unconscious.'

Miranda gave her an urgent, inquiring look.

'Get behind the door,' Holly whispered to her two friends. 'And wait for my signal.'

The study door opened a few centimetres then stopped.

'Claire?' they heard Tessa call.

'Yes?' came Claire's voice from above.

'See if those kids know where the drummer is!' shouted Tessa. 'We'll take that as well!'

'OK,' Claire called down.

During that brief exchange, Holly, Peter and Miranda crammed themselves into cover behind the door. Bethany sprawled on the floor, the bottle of pills open, capsules spilling out.

Tessa gave a sharp hiss of breath as she saw the young girl lying on the study floor.

She walked towards her, coming to a halt on the carpet, just as Holly had hoped she would.

For long, agonising moments she stood over Bethany, looking down at her without moving.

Holly made silent gestures to Peter and Miranda, indicating her plan to grab the near end of the carpet and yank it out from under Tessa's feet.

Tessa crouched and reached out to touch Bethany's shoulder.

'Are you OK?' said Tessa. 'Can you hear me?'

Bethany let out a very realistic groan.

135

'How many has she taken, I wonder?' murmured Tessa, obviously speaking to herself. She reached down and picked up bottles of pills. 'Silly girl,' she said. 'I'm afraid I haven't got the time to call an ambulance for you. You'd just better hope someone finds you before it's too late.'

Holly gave a sharp nod and the three of them pounced forwards. They grabbed hold of the tassled end of the carpet and wrenched at it with all their combined strength.

Tessa was taken completely by surprise. The carpet slipped from under her on the polished floorboards and she was catapulted on to her face.

'Cover her over!' yelled Holly. 'Quick!'

Bethany scuttled out of the way as the three friends threw the carpet over Tessa's head.

Tessa was flattened into the floor as their combined weight came down on top of her. She let out a stifled shriek which broke off suddenly as Bethany sat on her head.

'So you were just going to leave me to die of an overdose, were you?' howled Bethany, bouncing up and down on top of the woman as she struggled feebly under the carpet. 'I'll teach *you!*'

Holly and the others rolled the carpet and tucked it under itself, cocooning Tessa in a tight roll.

'Can we tie it with anything?' gasped Miranda.

'I've got an idea,' panted Bethany. She ran to a heavy padded leather armchair and started dragging it over towards the others.

Peter helped her and between them they managed to tip the chair forwards over the writhing carpet roll. From within they could hear muffled gasps and shouts. There was a yelp from Tessa as the weight of the upended armchair came down over her, pinning her to the floor.

'Now for Creepy Crawly!' exclaimed Bethany. 'I'm going to enjoy getting my own back on *her!*'

'Careful, Bethany,' said Holly as the young girl ran for the door. 'She'll have heard us!'

The three Mystery Kids pelted after Bethany. The girl came to a floundering halt halfway up the stairs. Claire was at the top, glaring down at them with a ferocious expression on her face. Her bright red mouth twisted in anger as she began to descend towards them.

Miranda leaped at a tall coat stand that stood by the hall cabinet.

'Come on!' she yelled. 'Help me!'

She grabbed the stand and dragged it towards the stairs. Holly and Peter cottoned on immediately. They ran up behind her, each grabbing a section of the coat stand. The three of them went charging up the stairs, wielding the wooden stand like a battering-ram.

'Duck, Bethany!' yelled Miranda.

Bethany dived out of the way as the three of them stampeded past her.

Claire gave a single high-pitched shriek as the top of the coat stand caught her right in the middle and she was sent stumbling backwards.

She came up against a closed door with a breathless gasp, the wind knocked completely out of her.

'Get her!' yelled Bethany.

'We've got her!' gasped Miranda. 'It's OK! We've got her!'

Holly saw Claire squirming and trying to

reach behind herself. A moment later the door they'd pinned her against fell open. Claire jumped backwards into the room and snatched the door closed.

Holly tripped over her own feet and the three of them came tumbling down on the landing.

'Don't let her get away!' Peter shouted as he tried to get up. His leg got tangled up in the stand and he collapsed on top of Miranda.

'She can't get away!' shouted Bethany. 'She's shut herself in the bathroom.'

Holly staggered to her feet. 'Hey!' she called, banging on the bathroom door. 'You show so much as your nose out here and we'll knock the stuffing out of you!'

There was no response from within the locked room. One thing was pretty obvious: at that moment the very last thing Claire had in mind was confronting three angry Mystery Kids armed with a hard and very heavy coat stand.

'You keep watch,' said Bethany. 'I've got an idea!'

She went tearing up the stairs.

'Phew!' said Miranda, pushing Peter off

her and sitting up. She grinned. 'That's both of them sorted out! We've done it, Holly!' She grimaced as she looked down at herself. 'Peter, for heaven's sake! Look at this, you've got jam all over me! It's come off your sleeve!'

'I'm *so* sorry,' said Peter. 'Send me the cleaning bill, why don't you? I mean, I really *asked* to have that junk tipped all over me!' He looked at Holly. 'One of us should call the police. Like, *now*!'

'You go,' said Holly. 'We'll keep watch over her.'

'No need!' shouted Bethany as she came running back down the stairs. 'We can make sure she can't get out.'

She was carrying a big ball of thick string. She tied one end to the bathroom door handle and then wound the ball round and round the banister rail before taking it back to the door and tying it to the handle again.

'Ha!' she said, banging the door with her palm. 'Let's see you get out of *that*, Creepy Crawly! You're going to pay for what you did to my dad!'

'It was Tessa!' came a feeble whining voice

from behind the door. 'It wasn't my idea. It was all Tessa's idea, right from the start. She made me do it. She made me give your father the sleeping pills. I never wanted to do it.'

The four friends looked at one another.

'What a weed!' said Bethany.

A dull thud sounded from the study.

'We'd better get down there,' said Peter. 'It sounds like Tessa's trying to get free.'

Before anyone had the chance to move there was a second loud thud.

'Oh, crumbs!' breathed Miranda. 'That sounded like the chair.'

'Listen,' came Claire's whinging voice through the door. 'Let me out and I promise I'll tell the police all about Tessa's plan. I'll confess everything!'

'You snivelling wretch!' It was Tessa. She came staggering out of the study, looking tousled and dishevelled and very, very angry. She leaned heavily on the banister rail. It had obviously taken her a lot of energy to fight her way out of the prison they had made for her.

'Don't you come near us!' shouted Holly.

Tessa lifted her arm and they saw something long and thin gleaming in her hand.

'Watch out!' gasped Miranda. 'She's got a knife!'

**Case closed**

For a few moments Holly and the others stood frozen in fear as Tessa stared up at them, her weapon pointing towards them up the stairs.

Then Bethany let out a cry. 'It's not a knife,' she said. 'It's only a letter-opener.'

'It's sharp enough,' warned Tessa, brandishing the letter-opener up towards them. 'It's sharp enough to damage anyone who tries to stop me.'

There was a thump on the bathroom door and the rattle of the handle.

'Tessa! Help me!' shouted Claire from the bathroom. 'You can't just leave me!'

'Can't I?' said Tessa. 'We'll see about that. Give my regards to the police when they get here.'

Still holding the letter-opener towards the

four of them, Tessa began to back along the hallway.

Holly tried desperately to think of some way of stopping her. They had Claire, and they had all the evidence they needed to prove to the police what had been going on. But unless they acted quickly there was still the chance that Tessa Burke would escape.

She came to the front door, her eyes fixed on them as she groped behind herself for the door latch.

The four of them, with Holly in the lead, started to move slowly down the stairs.

'Keep back!' snarled Tessa.

They could now see something that Tessa couldn't. Behind her a shadow had moved across the door's frosted glass panels.

'Look behind you,' Miranda called in a sing-song voice.

'Don't be so stupid!' spat Tessa.

'She's not kidding,' said Holly. 'I'd really take a look behind you, if I were you.'

Tessa let out a wordless snarl as her fingers finally found the latch and she pulled the door open.

*Whack*! The door sprang open, pushed

hard from outside. With a whoop of shock, Tessa went flying forwards, the letter-opener spinning out of her hand.

A burly police officer shoved his way into the hallway. Holly could see a couple of other men behind him in the porch.

Before Tessa knew what had hit her, the three Mystery Kids came leaping down the rest of the stairs and caught hold of her. They pulled her to the ground and pinned her arms to her sides as she struggled.

'Dad!' shouted Bethany, running down the stairs.

Sure enough, one of the men who followed the police officer into the house was Maurice Harty. And as he saw Tessa and the four youngsters the expression on his face was one of pure disbelief.

'We've got Claire locked up in the bathroom,' said Holly. 'They were in it together!'

'Dad! You never stole that model!' shouted Bethany as she threw her arms round her father. 'And you weren't having blackouts! They gave you sleeping-pills!'

'I don't . . . what? . . . I . . .' Maurice Harty stared round as if in a dream.

'Don't worry,' said Holly with a big grin. 'We can explain the whole thing.'

'I'd be glad if you would,' said the third man, stepping from behind Bethany and her father. 'I'm Detective Sergeant Rollins. Mr Harty here has just informed us of a serious crime which he committed.' He looked sternly at the Mystery Kids. 'So now would one of you like to explain to me what the bright blue blazes is going on here?'

It was several days later. The Mystery Kids were back in their office in Peter's house. Miranda was perched on the windowsill with her feet tucked under her. Peter was leaning over Holly, who was sitting at the desk and writing.

She was finishing an article for *The Tom-tom*. It was called 'Operation Save John Raven.'

'How's this, then?' she said, and she read aloud as she wrote. '"This was when we discovered where Maurice Harty had been all that time while we were battling with Tessa Burke and Claire Crawley."'

'Did you mention that Peter was smelling like a compost heap?' interrupted Miranda.

'She did,' said Peter. 'Several times.'

Miranda grinned. 'Good. We wouldn't want to miss that out.'

'You wouldn't, you mean,' said Peter. 'I'd rather forget all about it. I was washing tea leaves out of my hair for three days!'

'Just listen, will you?' said Holly. 'Where was I? Oh, yes. "It turned out that after he had put the envelope with the money in it in the tree he had a—",' She stopped, sucking her pen. 'What should we put?'

'A crisis of conscience,' said Peter. 'Put that.'

'What does it mean?' asked Miranda.

'It means he felt really bad about not going to the police about the robbery he thought he'd committed,' said Peter. 'It means that instead of going straight home that final day, he went to the police station to give himself up and confess.'

'Fine,' said Holly, writing again. '"He had a crisis of conscience and told the police about the robbery. Which was why Maurice and the police arrived at exactly the right moment to stop Tessa Burke escaping. Just

147

like in *Spyglass*, the best television programme ever. I then explained to Detective Inspector Rollins—"'

'Detective *Sergeant* Rollins,' said Peter.

'Yes, OK, OK,' Holly said impatiently.

'And what's all this "I" business? We *all* explained it to him.'

'All right,' sighed Holly, crossing out the 'I' and putting in 'we'. '"We then explained to blah-blah-blah about the blackmailing that had been going on and how the two women had set the whole thing up."'

'"Criminal women,"' said Peter.

'"Horrible, nasty, ghastly criminal women,"' added Miranda. 'I think we could do with a few good adjectives here.'

'Fine,' said Holly. 'I'll stick in as many adjectives as you like.' She carried on writing. '"And then Claire was let out of the bathroom and she confessed everything, like the complete weed we all knew she was."' Holly smiled. '"Thereby,"' she wrote grandly, '"proving that our theory about the theft of the drummer boy and the sleeping tablets and *everything* was completely, totally and utterly correct!"'

148

There was a knock on the door and Peter's father's voice came from outside.

'We should be going now, gang,' he said. 'You don't want to keep the stars waiting!'

Holly looked at her watch. She hadn't noticed how quickly the time had passed.

'Coming!' called Peter.

The three friends made a run for the door. In an hour's time they were supposed to be at the television studio where *Spyglass* was being filmed.

Maurice Harty had arranged for them to have a behind-the-scenes guided tour of the set during filming of an actual episode of *Spyglass*. And then they were being taken to dinner at a posh restaurant with all the regular cast members.

It was hardly surprising that they were in a state of manic excitement as they chased one another down the stairs and jostled for seats in Mr Hamilton's car.

Not only had they saved Maurice Harty from the clutches of two ruthless and wicked women, but their reward was the most exciting thing they could think of in the entire world. To actually be there in the television

149

studio to see their hero Secret Agent John Raven in action.

Just before they had left their office, Holly had scribbled a final note at the end of the article for *The Tom-tom*.

*Case closed! The Mystery Kids have done it again!*

Hodder Children's Books

**Another Hodder Children's book**

*Fiona Kelly*

**SPY-CATCHERS!
THE MYSTERY KIDS 1**

*You can't keep a secret from these three!*

London is teeming with spies –
and Holly and Miranda are just the
people to catch them.

All they need is practice. Who is the
sinister man lurking outside Holly's
house? What does Miranda's mother
*really* do for the government?

Then they spot a suspicious-
looking boy – and the real mystery
begins . . .

Hodder
Children's
Books

## Another Hodder Children's book

*Fiona Kelly*

## LOST AND FOUND
## THE MYSTERY KIDS 2

*A ticket to adventure*

Holly's desperate for a mystery to solve – and when she sees a ferrety-looking man throw his wallet from the bus, she knows she's found one!

Peter and Miranda aren't so sure. The wallet is empty when they go back to find it. Empty except for some sort of ticket – and there's nothing mysterious about that . . . or is there?

**Hodder Children's Books**

# Another Hodder Children's book

*Fiona Kelly*

## TREASURE HUNT
## THE MYSTERY KIDS 3

*On the trail of a lost fortune*

What happens when you've got
no crime to solve? You look for an
unsolved crime!

The Mystery Kids read about a
blackmail attempt that happened
years earlier. The criminal was
arrested – but the money was never
found! Now Holly, Miranda and
Peter are in pursuit of a suitcase full
of cash.

Trouble is, the Mystery Kids aren't
the only ones looking . . .

## THE MYSTERY KIDS SERIES
## FIONA KELLY

| 61989 9 | SPY-CATCHERS!    | £2.99 ☐ |
| 61990 2 | LOST AND FOUND   | £2.99 ☐ |
| 61991 0 | TREASURE HUNT    | £2.99 ☐ |
| 61992 9 | THE EMPTY HOUSE  | £2.99 ☐ |
| 61993 7 | SMUGGLERS BAY    | £2.99 ☐ |
| 61994 5 | FUNNY MONEY      | £2.99 ☐ |
| 65356 6 | BLACKMAIL!       | £2.99 ☐ |
| 65565 8 | MYSTERY WEEKEND  | £2.99 ☐ |
| 65566 6 | WRONG NUMBER     | £2.99 ☐ |
| 65567 4 | HOSTAGE          | £2.99 ☐ |
| 65568 2 | BOX OF TRICKS    | £2.99 ☐ |
| 65569 0 | KIDNAP!          | £2.99 ☐ |

*All Hodder Children's books are available at your local bookshop or newsagent, or can be ordered direct from the publisher. Just tick the titles you want and fill in the form below. Prices and availability subject to change without notice.*

Hodder Children's Books, Cash Sales Department, Bookpoint, 39 Milton Park, Abingdon, OXON, OX14 4TD, UK. If you have a credit card you may order by telephone – 01235 831700.

Please enclose a cheque or postal order may payable to Bookpoint Ltd to the value of the cover price and allow the following for postage and packing: UK & BFPO:- £1.00 for the first book, 50p for the second book, and 30p for each additional book ordered up to a maximum charge of £3.00.
OVERSEAS & EIRE:- £2.00 for the first book, £1.00 for the second book, and 50p for each additional book.

Name ......................................................................................................................

Address ..................................................................................................................

................................................................................................................................

................................................................................................................................

If you would prefer to pay by credit card, please complete:
Please debit my Visa/Access/Diner's Card/American Express (delete as applicable) card no:

| | | | | | | | | | | | | | | | |
|---|---|---|---|---|---|---|---|---|---|---|---|---|---|---|---|

Signature ...............................................................................................................

Expiry Date ...........................................................................................................